Walking Out of the Canadian Wilderness

George Wright
Also from Second Wind Publishing
Novels by George Wright

Yaweta
Runaway
Redstone

www.secondwindpublishing.com

Walking Out of the Canadian Wilderness

By

George Wright

Savage Books
Published by Second Wind Publishing, LLC.
Kernersville

George Wright

Savage Books
Second Wind Publishing, LLC
931-B South Main Street, Box 145
Kernersville, NC 27284

First Savage Books edition published
March 2014
Savage Books, Running Angel, and all production design are trademarks of Second Wind Publishing, used under license.

For information regarding bulk purchases of this book, digital purchase and special discounts, please contact the publisher at
www.secondwindpublishing.com

Cover design by Stacy Castanedo

Manufactured in the United States of America
ISBN 978-1-938101-63-2

In Memory of George Wright,
Patriot, Scholar, Author

George Wright

CHAPTER 1

The airplane left the International Airport in Ireland bound for Vancouver, British Columbia at precisely the right time. The pilot reported ideal flight conditions for the entire voyage. Josh Mcdougal was seated mid-ship one seat away from the window.

He had just settled into his seat for flight 6969 when the passenger that had the window seat came to sit. Josh noticed immediately that she was beautiful and well-endowed. He felt almost an electric current go through him as he rose to allow her into her seat. To him she was the ideal woman. He introduced himself, but she only said her name, "Mary McIntosh," and pulled out a book to read. Josh took the hint and went to work on his laptop computer. He was used to it. He was just an ordinary person of medium height, not good-looking nor ugly, just ordinary in every respect. There was no reason a beauty such as was sitting beside him would notice him at all.

Flight 6969 had no problems until they were passing over the Canadian wilderness. Something caused the airplane to jerk violently. The pilot looked to his left and witnessed the left jets and part of the wing float away and fall. He got on the radio and tried to call in to let people know what had happened, but the radio had been damaged. The wiring of that particular model of aircraft was such that some it routed through the wing so the radio was now actually disconnected from its power source. He could handle the craft, but had to descend from 30,000 feet down to 10,000. This put him below the radar so he dropped off the screen, and soon there were reports of his craft being down. What was reported was the wing and two jets. Rescue crafts were dispatched, but no airplane was found.

Ten thousand feet was a safe altitude if he did not encounter any tall mountains. There was a strong wind at that altitude, and it blew the aircraft off course and north. There was nothing the pilot could do but hope for a landing strip somewhere. He had

1

little power in his remaining engines against the wind. The craft was going slow and laboring as he nursed it along. Eventually the remaining jet engines overheated and forced him to make a crash landing. The fifty-seven passengers prepared with their heads down and ready.

The pilot saw the only place he could bring the airplane down and still have a chance to save at least some of his passengers. It was what appeared to be a flat-topped mountain. Appearances are deceiving. The clearing he was trying to land on was only about fifty yards wide. Thick forest was on the other side.

The plane crashed across the clearing and into the forest as though landing. Big trees ripped off what little was left of the damaged wing and the other wing. Fuel from the wing tanks drenched the fuselage. The body of the craft skidded over rocks and logs. Josh and Mary were sitting next to the emergency exit. When it flew open, something separated the two seats the couple occupied. They skidded across an open area and up a slight rise, coming to rest almost upside down.

Shaken, with their clothing ripped, but otherwise relatively unhurt except for some scrapes and bruises, they remained locked in their seats. Mary's skirt went way up, revealing her shapely legs and her dainty bikini panties. Her blouse and bra were ripped open, and one breast was completely exposed. Josh of course noticed and even noted that she was a natural redhead. He also observed that her breasts were large and beautifully shaped with large areolae and nipples.

He undid the clasp of his seatbelt and tumbled out onto the ground. He then reached and popped the clasp on hers, catching her as she fell. They stood and watched as the fuselage burst into flame, engulfing everything, including any other survivors of the crash. Mary cried out and, in her shock and grief, came into Josh's arms. He held her, only semi-conscious of her breasts pressing against him. They watched the demise of the other passengers and the crew, unable to keep from looking. Fortunately, they could not actually see any of them nor hear any sound because of the noise made by the flames.

2

As the shock subsided, Mary noticed she was in the man's arms and pushed away. She saw that her breast was exposed and turned as red as her hair. Josh acted as though he had not noticed. He looked toward the wreck and observed her out of the corner of his eye. If she noticed the bulge in his pants, she never said anything.

Once she had herself decent, Josh turned and told her, "We best stick around here for a while in case they send someone after us. The craft is equipped with an emergency locater. I hope that it survived the fire. In the meantime, we need something to keep us warm. It is late in the day, and I am sure there will be no rescue until morning at least."

There was no point in trying to search the wreckage since everything burned so they backtracked the crash site, finding luggage that had been in the hold of the airplane. At one point they found a couple of blankets. They were the type the airline used and must have been in use at the time of the crash and been sucked out of the airplane during the crash. They found a suitcase with clothes that would fit Josh and another with women's clothes that Mary could wear. One bag was a duffel bag similar to that used in the military. It had a long strap so it could be slung over a person's shoulder for hands-free carrying. Josh emptied it and folded it up in case they needed it. Each of them went in opposite directions to change out of their torn and ruined garments. Nothing else was of use to them at the time, so they returned to the wreckage, each with a few extra clothes.

Back at the pair of seats, he put the extra clothes in the duffel and hung it on a broken branch. He was able to pull the two seats close to the heat of the hot metal that was once their transportation. By then it was nearly dark so he spread a blanket over each seat, folded in half. The mechanism to recline the back still worked so he leaned them back as far as they would go. They covered themselves and settled down for the night, each wrapped in a blanket.

Two hours later Josh was awake. He was quite cold in the mountain's night air. He could see in the moonlight that Mary was shivering but still fitfully sleeping. He got up, pulled her half blanket off, spread it over his chair, and sat down again. He used his blanket to cover both of them so that their body heat would keep both of them warm. Before long, he was sleeping, and she was no longer shivering.

At dawn Josh opened his eyes to discover that at some point during the night, she had cuddled up close to him, and he had his arm around her in an embrace. He heard a quiet noise that sounded for the entire world like a kitten purring. It was her making the sound.

He came out of the fog of sleep becoming more and more aware of their situation. He began to think about what had to be done. He had to locate that emergency locater and make sure it was working. That would be first and then some food for the lady. He hoped something had survived the fire.

As he started to remove his arm from around her and get out of bed, she awoke. She jumped up and went into a tirade about him trying to get fresh with her. She noticed the new arrangement of the blankets. She became even angrier, berating him for being so forward and assuming she was "that type of woman." She accused him of molesting her in her sleep and trying to rape her. She called him a dirty pervert and a few other names that no lady should even know.

Josh ignored her outburst and walked out into the forest to relieve his bladder. When he returned, she was still mouthing off. He went to the wreckage and started searching. He found the locater to be a molten mass of metal so he knew it was not working. Both flight recorders were intact so he set them out so they could be found easily. He hoped there was a locater built into the black boxes but knew that was doubtful. Their purpose was to record flight data, not let the authorities know the craft's location.

He kicked open a refrigerator door and found some prepared lunches and a few cans of juice. He brought them over to where she sat and put them down. He could tell she was still pouting.

He told her, "Miss, here's food. Eat!" They sat down and ate their first meal since the crash. Josh thought, *This is the first time I ever ate airline food that tasted good.* He told her about the locater and suggested they stick around the wreckage for a day to see if anyone had noticed the smoke from the fire.

She asked, "What if they didn't?"

Josh replied, "Well, Miss, I guess then we will have to walk out of here." With a snort of disgust, she indicated her opinion that they could never walk to civilization. Around noon Josh decided they had better prepare for night.

He told her, "Unless you want to sleep with me again tonight, we had better find some more covers; it gets cold at night at this elevation."

Mary actually smiled as they went looking. Of course, she waited until Josh would not be able to see her. They did find their own luggage and rummaged through them to get some of their personal things. Josh wished he had packed something besides suits. He had been on a lecture tour, and more substantial clothing was not necessary. The soft cloth would not last long if they had to move through brush and up and down hills. Mary had her purse, and it contained her toothbrush, comb and some makeup. In one bag Josh found a pair of work boots that fit him nicely. In that same bag, he discovered a genuine Bowie knife with both sides of the blade honed razor sharp, complete in a scabbard. It was easily fourteen inches in length and built heavy. Josh was thrilled about getting such a valuable tool. The same suitcase contained blue jeans and flannel shirts. The traveler who owned these things must have been a working man. He found a roll of fishing line that he promptly put in his pocket. In several bags he found things he did not need stored in plastic bags. He dumped the contents and put the bags in his pockets.

Mary knew she needed more comfortable shoes if she were going to go traipsing off into the woods. She found a pair of hiking boots that fit and some women's jeans. Josh pocketed three cigarette lighters he found and then tossed her a couple of shirts that would fit her. Still hoping for a rescue, she only carried the things along because "that man" told her to do so. They did not find any more blankets.

On the way back to the wreckage, Josh found one of the

5

toilet seats from the airplane. He picked it up and told her he would go rig a place for it in case it was needed for its obvious purpose. He went out, put together some fallen timber, and placed the seat so it could be used.

As he returned, he noticed a concave piece of wing about six feet by eight feet in size. It was about fifty yards from where he had placed their bed/seats. He went to it and, with great difficulty, pulled it over to the temporary camp spot near the wreckage. He propped it against some trees and turned the seats to face it. He built a fire between the seats and the piece of wing. He gathered dead wood for the night, and they sat down in the chairs to eat the last of the airplane fare.

While they ate, Josh explained why he had changed their sleeping arrangement the night before. "We needed each other's body heat to stay warm." They still had two small cans of juice when they finished their repast. Josh said they should save them, just in case.

Mary went into the woods and changed into the jeans and one of the shirts she had found in their foraging. Upon return, she spread the blankets across both seats and got under the covers. Josh took his place beside her.

She told him, "You might as well call me by my given name. *Miss* sounds so formal. By the way, keeping warm was no excuse for having your arm around me last night." He heard her quiet giggle.

She commented on how the piece of wing reflected the heat from the fire. She asked, "How did you know to do that?"

He said, "Lucky guess" and left it at that.

They slept warm. Josh got up now and then and put more wood on the fire. During the night it snowed enough to cover the ground about an inch. They awoke to a cold morning. Josh told her, "We have to get off this mountain, or we will freeze before we starve or die of thirst." She was not in a good mood. She was cold, miserable and scared.

Mary said, "We are going to die anyway, aren't we? Here or in the woods, what difference does it make?"

Josh assured her, "We will not die. We are well- equipped

and will go down this mountain to a lower elevation where it is warmer. There we will find a stream for water and food for our bellies. We will follow that stream down until it joins another and that one until it joins yet another. We will find civilization eventually."

She retorted, "Well-equipped? We have nothing on which to survive, and you are a fool for thinking so. If you think I am traipsing off into the woods with you, you are sadly mistaken. Don't think I don't know you were being fresh with me again last night either." She stomped off into the woods, only to return a few minutes later.

Josh blushed. He had purposely put his arm around her and pulled her closer. He had fondled one of her breasts briefly, but that was more by accident than on purpose, although he had enjoyed it.

While she was gone, Josh pulled the piece of wing into a different position and aimed it carefully so it would reflect the sun.

Mary sat on her seat bed with her arms crossed. Josh began to break camp and load the duffel for their journey. Once their meager possessions were loaded, he kicked the fire around and stomped on the embers to put them out. He hoisted the duffel on his shoulder and asked, "Are you ready to go?"

CHAPTER 2

Mary never said a word, just stared off into space. Josh shrugged his shoulders and started out. He went about a hundred yards and stopped. It was the clearing on which the pilot was trying to land their airplane. He could see the skid marks and the devastation the crash had caused. He leaned against a tree and waited.

Mary sat there for a while and suddenly realized Josh was gone, and she was all alone. In her mind she blamed herself. Her temper and doubt, combined with fright, had driven him away. Fear caused her to put on the shoes and socks Josh has carefully set out for her to wear. She was already dressed in jeans and a boy's shirt. She started after Josh in the direction she thought she saw him enter the woods. She had not gone far when she became very confused about directions. She could not see the wreckage anymore and was completely lost, so the fear turned to panic. She began to run as panicked people tend to do. Fortunately for her, she ran in the right direction.

As Mary entered the clearing, she stopped, completely out of breath. Her eyes were wide and dilated as she searched around. Josh stepped out from the tree he was leaning against and asked, "Did you decide to come along?" She squealed and jumped into his arms.

She held him tight and told him, "I was so scared and I panicked. Please don't ever leave me again. I'll do whatever you ask; just don't leave me again."

He told her, "We better get moving, or we will never make it off this mountain today. I want to be near a stream before dark." He gave her no comfort or assurance. She needed the lesson he hoped she had learned.

Knowing they had a long day ahead of them, he went at a leisurely pace across the clearing and started the descent. They were obliged to detour around deadfall and outcroppings, but steadily descended. Sometimes they were obliged to climb down the face of a low cliff.

Around noon they stopped to rest. They finished the last two small cans of juice while sitting on a downed log. Mary was about to throw her can away when Josh stopped her. "Don't throw that away; it will come in handy when we reach good water." He put the two empty cans in the duffel.

The ground had been disturbed at one spot, and Mary saw a track in the dirt. She asked what kind of animal had made the track. He looked and said it was nothing but a cat. It was actually the track of a cougar, but he did not want another case of paranoid fear. She had suffered enough traumas.

Along the way, they came across a patch of blueberry and huckleberry bushes. Josh told her, "We had better stop and eat some of these berries. They could be all we have to eat today."

She scoffed at him and said, "How do you know they are not poisonous or would make us sick? I do not want to eat something dangerous like that."

He told her, "I'll eat a few, and if I drop dead, you will know, so then do not eat any."

He thought to himself, *She better learn to trust me soon, or this is going to be one tedious trip.*

Josh was wearing a hat he had found in one of the suitcases so he took it off and filled it with berries. They ate until Josh saw a bear approaching from the other side of the patch. He told her they had enough and needed to get moving. She heard the bear grunt and asked, "What was that noise?"

He told her, "Just a harmless animal like a squirrel."

The slope became very steep so Josh started switch backing. He led them back and forth downward so as to make the walk easier. Once she noticed their zigzagging, she complained that they should walk straight down. He told her to go ahead if she wanted to do that. She took three steps and fell on her rump. She slid about ten feet before coming against a tree that broke her momentum. She got up and held on to the tree, not saying a word as she rubbed her butt. Josh heard no more arguments out of her for a while.

They came to the top of a high rimrock. As Mary warned him to be careful, Josh leaned out and looked both directions,

9

turned right and walked along the top of the rimrock until it petered out. They slipped and slid down to a path that ran below the rimrocks. They walked along the bottom of the cliff and finally down a game trail which took them to a stream. It was late in the afternoon so Josh said they would camp there for the night.

CHAPTER 3

He chose a place away from the stream in a small opening surrounded by forest. She watched as he worked to set up camp. Josh carefully went over a patch of ground, removing sticks and stones. He used his knife to loosen the soil before placing the blankets over the spot. Mary watched with questioning eyes but said nothing. She was beginning to learn. Once it was set up, he cleared another area of pine needles and other debris, dug a hole and piled the dirt on one side of the hole. He built a small campfire in the hole.

Josh excused himself and said he had something to do, but he would be back shortly. Mary told him, "Please don't be gone long, and don't go so far you get lost." He told her he would try and left. He was gone nearly half an hour before he returned. Mary was worried because it had seemed like hours to her.

He took the "privy" seat with him and set up that "necessity" as he did every time they camped. He had other things to do as well. He set some snares along a rabbit run and went fishing. It did not take long.

When he returned, he was carrying two clumps of mud he had gotten from the stream. He put them in the campfire and scraped live coals over them. He went to the stream and filled their two empty juice cans with water. He put more wood on the fire and sat beside Mary. She asked him, "Why in the world did you put those big piles of mud in the fire and cover them?"

He told her, "You will see after a bit."

They talked about their journey down the mountainside for a while.

Eventually she told him why she was on the airplane. She had been the executive assistant to the CEO of a large corporation. She quit because of sexual harassment. She had been told to sleep with her boss or go to the "steno pool." She had been going on vacation before she sought another position with a more traditional company.

Josh told her he was kind of a bum and was going home

after a long trip. He did not elaborate. He was enjoying her company and was somewhat of a tease. She asked what he did for work so he told her, "Mostly nothing, but I do teach school now and then."

Eventually Josh told her, "I hope you like fish" as he pulled the two lumps out of the fire. Each lump of mud was now hard, and when he broke them open, they each contained two trout about a foot long. While they were eating, she asked where he got the fish. With a twinkle in his eyes he told her, "From the fish market just downstream." He did not tell her he caught them with his bare hands. She hit his shoulder and told him she did not believe that for a minute. He then told her they were stuck in the mud, and he just picked them up. She let it go, but she had a lot more appreciation for Josh McDougal after that.

After finishing their fish, they ate berries. Josh took the few that were left over after they were satisfied and scattered them about the clearing. She asked why, and he told her it was for the little creatures. He did not tell her a passing bear might want them. Scattered, they might take root and grow. Someday another wanderer might eat some and perhaps survive in the harsh wilderness.

The night was cold, and Mary had no problem with cuddling close to Josh for warmth even before they went to sleep. Josh had a difficult time sleeping with her so close. His arm went around her to pull her even closer as they spooned back to front. After he dozed off, his hand moved up from her waist to her breasts. She moaned a little in her sleep and crossed her arm over his so that his hand was trapped on her breast. Josh woke when she moaned and noticed what had happened. He was awake most of the night.

Josh woke early, got a fire going and slipped out of camp. A while later he came back with a rabbit. The snares he had set worked. The fish line he salvaged from a suitcase made a good snare. When Mary woke up, he was roasting the meat over the fire. She asked, "Where did you get that?" She asked what it was and told him she had never eaten rabbit. He told her she would like it because it tasted like chicken. Then he told her he

12

called out for delivery service. He said he thought they should eat something with substance since they had a long way to travel. She told him he should have ordered a taxicab when he ordered the delivery.

He responded, "No, I didn't want to ruin our holiday in the woods."

Mary sat silent for a long time. She was beginning to realize that there was a lot more to this virtual stranger than she at first surmised. She said, "You have been camping in the woods before, haven't you?"

He told her, "A couple of times. We had better get a move on; we are wasting daylight."

As they moved along, she looked at him and said, "I noticed that you have not shaved since the wreck. You do not have a beard of any kind, not even stubble. Why is that?"

He told her, "I have never shaved in my life. For some reason I just do not grow a beard. I think it is a throwback to some of my American Indian ancestors."

CHAPTER 4

They followed a path various animals had made parallel to the stream. At one point it turned and crossed the water. Josh picked Mary up and carried her across so she would not get her feet wet. He set her down on the other side and went back into the stream. She watched as he reached down into the water beside a big rock. He went from one to the other and felt around. He suddenly flipped his arm toward her and something flew past her.

She turned and saw a large fish flopping on the grass behind her. Josh came out of the stream, picked up the fish and began to clean it in the water. Once the fish was gutted and cleaned out, he wrapped it in leaves, put it inside a plastic bag and stored it in the duffel. He looked at her and said, "That's our lunch." Mary's admiration for the man grew.

Eventually the game trail left the stream so they continued without it. They traveled away from the stream about fifty or sixty feet because there was much less underbrush. Willows and cottonwood trees were thick next to the water. Once in a while there was an opening so they could go get water in their cans. Sometimes a cliff or other obstruction would block one side or the other, so it was necessary to cross over and walk on the other side. Josh always carried her across.

Eventually it had to happen. A rock rolled under Josh's foot, and they both went down. They were not hurt because the depth of the water broke their fall. They walked out of the water soaked to the skin. Fortunately Josh had already taken the duffel across so they had dry clothing.

While Mary went off to change and do whatever she needed, Josh built a campfire in the same manner as the previous one. He used green willow branches and built a rack, covered it with cottonwood leaves and then filleted the fish and put the meat on the leaves. He then covered the fish with leaves and set the whole thing over the fire propped up on forked sticks about a foot over the hot coals.

He asked Mary to watch the cooking while he went off to change. They hung their wet clothes on branches to dry, and once the fish was cooked, sat down to eat. Mary was impressed that it tasted so good.

As she stirred about, Josh caught glimpses of her bra through a gap in her shirt where she had forgotten to fasten a button. He suddenly hit his forehead with the palm of his hand and said, "How dumb can a man be? Here I have been wishing I had a sling shot, and there you are wearing one." She looked at him as though she thought he had gone crazy.

He told her, "Remove your bra and give it to me. I need it to make my slingshot."

She refused, "I most certainly will not. Do you think I want to go without my bra? You must be mad."

He reminded her, "Remember you told me you would do anything I said. I need that bra, or I would not ask."

She still refused, "That is not fair and no, that is final."

He told her, "Take it off or I will do it for you." She saw the look in his eyes and knew he would do it. She went into the trees and came back with the garment in her hand. "Here, I hope you are satisfied."

Mary's own game was not that she minded in the least bit having to give up her bra. It was uncomfortable and tight. She knew she could have given him the spare she had in the duffel, but that would not have been any fun.

He took his knife, cut the straps away, and fashioned a sling shot using the elastic and a forked stick. He found some pebbles and practiced. She was impressed with his marksmanship, but unimpressed with his new weapon. He told her, "This is going to help us eat." She could not see how a toy slingshot would do anything.

By this time it was getting late in the day, and the clothes were not yet dry. Josh told her they might as well camp there so started preparing the site for their night. Once everything was done, she told him, "Why don't you take your new toy out and see if we have to fast or eat tonight?"

The way she said "toy" made it sound as though she was a

little disgusted with the idea of it. Josh said he thought he would just do that very thing. He left and was gone an hour. She was panicking with worry when he came back with two birds all dressed and feathered. They looked like small chickens to her. She asked, "Where in the world did you find chickens out here?"

He told her, "These are grouse, and I shot them with my toy." When she wanted to know what a grouse tasted like, he told her, "Chicken." They roasted the birds and ate a fine meal.

After dinner, the wind shifted a little. It did not bother them because it was only a slight breeze, but a foul odor permeated the camp for a few moments. Josh recognized the smell of skunk, but she had never had that experience. She asked, "What is that awful odor?"

Josh told her, "That is a Big Foot, or as some say, Sasquatch. We will have no trouble from him, but all the animals will keep away from him because he scares them."

She asked if he might attack them. He told her they were vegetarian and would not attack a human. He said, "Probably because we are too much like them."

"What do you mean?" she asked.

He told her, "It is because they walk on two legs just as humans. There are some who believe they are a lost tribe of Indians. Others think they may be the missing link between man and ape."

She was not convinced so when it came time for bed, she was tight against him. His arm was around her, and her head used his shoulder as a pillow.

She sounded sleepy when she said, "You don't like me very much, do you." It was a statement, not a question.

He answered, "Oh, you are fine, just a little green to this kind of thing is all. You'll get along."

She muttered, "That is not what I asked," and he could feel her pull away from him a little. Josh was tired, since not having much sleep last night and carrying her across streams exhausted him. She was saying something when he drifted off to sleep.

When morning came, he discovered that they were as close

16

together as ever, and his left hand was holding her right breast over her shirt. He thought it certainly felt better without that damn bra.

It was an easy trail. The valley they were in widened a bit, and the terrain was less rugged. It began to feel like a walk in the park to Josh. He noticed she seemed to be getting along better. He led the way though a grove of lodge pole pine and was about to go out the other side when he suddenly stopped. Mary started to say something. He put his finger to his lips as a signal to be quiet. He motioned her to a thick clump of brush and signaled here to hide by putting his hands out and lowering them a couple of times. She caught on and did as he had signaled. He joined her.

A couple of minutes passed before she heard the snarls of an animal fight. Josh slowly moved forward with Mary behind him. He looked out from cover at the edge of the grove and witnessed a big wolf and a mountain lion contesting over a deer one of them had killed. It was a vicious fight, and either one could have bested the other, but if they had seen Josh and Mary, one or both could very well have attacked them. After a while, the wolf gave up and trotted off. The cougar latched onto his prize and drug it away. Josh waited about five minutes and told Mary, "Best we get on our way."

As they moved along, Josh noticed that the valley had begun to narrow again. The stream was narrower, and there were more rapids. Their trail had more of a downhill slope to it. He picked a spot and prepared for another night. Mary was worried about the cougar, but Josh told her, "There is no worry about the cat. His belly is full, and he will lay up for a couple of days. He will not bother us or anyone else until he gets hungry again." Nevertheless she was as close to him as she could get all night.

He was up, dressed, and off hunting long before she knew it was morning. When she woke up and saw he was gone, she panicked again. She knew in her mind that it was because she had confessed to him that she was very proud of him and the way he was taking care of her. She was saying that she had learned to trust him when she discovered that he was asleep. She thrust her fear away and went down to the stream to wash her face and try to make herself presentable for his return.

The water was as cold as ice and woke her up quickly. She realized she had brought nothing to dry her face and hands so she took off her shirt and used it as a towel. She had just finished with her face and was drying her hands when Josh came out of the trees near her.

He completely ignored the fact that she was nude from the waist up and said, "Good morning." He held up a rabbit and said, "I hope you don't mind rabbit again. I found some wild onions so I thought we could bake this one with the onions for a little variety."

When she saw him, she automatically started to cover her breasts, but his casual manner caused her to think again. She casually put on the shirt and asked, "How are you going to bake anything out here in the woods?"

He told her, "The same way we baked the fish that first time, only with a little twist. I will show you. There is some really good mud here, so why don't we prepare our meal for cooking right now?"

Her shirt was a little damp in just the right places to cause her nipples to extend and harden. Josh could see them poking her shirt out very nicely. He told her they needed leaves from a particular tree, a cottonwood, and she helped him gather much more than they needed.

Whenever she reached up to get some leaves, her breasts were plainly visible under her shirt with their pointing nipples. Josh enjoyed the view so much he let her pick most of the leaves and did not stop her until the pile was high, and he could see her arms were getting tired. She handed him the leaves, and he put them in the pile so he had a close-up view of what fascinated him.

Once the leaves were gathered, they cut up the onions and the rabbit and set them aside. They scattered some leaves and put mud on them about an inch thick. Then he put more leaves on top of the mud and the cut-up rabbit on that with the onions in and around the meat. More leaves and more mud made a large clump that would be their oven.

During the process, both of them got their shirts muddy. Josh took his shirt off and rinsed it out in the stream. He said, "Maybe you should wash your shirt too."

She told him, "I will as soon as you go back to camp and get me a dry shirt. I'll change while you put the meal in the fire."

Josh thought it was silly since he had already seen everything she would be exposing anyway. He told her, "Ok, whatever you wish, my dear."

As he left, she called out, "Would you bring me some clean pants as well? These are just as dirty as my shirt." He brought the requested garments and even some panties so she would have a complete change of clothing. She never thought about the fact that she was in plain sight of their camp as she changed. Josh enjoyed the entertainment.

CHAPTER 5

Josh watched and once again thought about her. She seemed to occupy his mind a lot. He knew he wanted her and knew he could probably seduce her or take her against her will. That was not the way he wanted her. He wanted her to willingly surrender herself to him. He knew he never had a chance of that happening. She was too beautiful and could choose any man in the world. She would not want him, and he did not want the heartache any other relationship would cause.

The meal was delicious, and she complimented him on his resourcefulness. She asked how he knew to cook that way. He told her he read it in a Boy Scout manual one time and just thought he would try it.

They packed up their gear and started down the trail after Josh obliterated the signs of their having camped there. She asked why he did that so he told her, "Always leave the woods as close to the way you found them as possible. The animals don't like us to leave their home dirty."

They found another game trail and followed it along the bank of the stream. Josh led the way some ten or so feet ahead of Mary, so when she stopped to curiously inspect the stump of a small tree, he did not notice. The stump looked as though something had chewed it down. About that time a small cottonwood fell across the path. If she had not stopped, it might have hit her. As she looked, she saw an animal rise up and look at her before scurrying off and diving into the water.

Of course she let out a bit of a squeal of surprise when the tree fell, and Josh heard. He asked if she were all right. She told him that the tree just startled her and described the animal. "I think it is the one that made the tree fall. Something has been cutting down these little trees, and it looks like tooth marks on the stumps."

He told her, "That is indeed true; it cut that tree and the others. It's called a 'lumberjack.'" Not knowing any different, she accepted his explanation.

They came to, and passed, the beaver dam. She saw the deep water and thought about how nice it would be if she could take a bath in that pond. She became conscious of the fact that she had not had a bath in days and probably would not have one for a long time yet. She called out to Josh, "How much longer do you think it will be before we find civilization? I need a bath."

Josh kept walking and said, "Until we get there." He knew he was being short with her, but his mind was on the scene she presented to him when she changed clothes. He could still see the patch of red hair at the junction of her beautifully shaped legs.

They camped again, and again they were on the uphill side of the stream. She asked him, "Why do we always camp up above the stream? It would be much easier if we were down close to the water."

He told her, "Two reasons. The animals come to the water to drink at night, and some are dangerous while others would be scared away. Secondly, it gets several degrees colder at night close to the chilly water. We are safer and warmer away from the stream."

He furnished her with two grouse again, and they each ate their fill. When they slept, she lay awake waiting for his comforting and sensuous hand on her breasts before she could go to sleep contented. She was sure she would capture his heart.

After fish for breakfast, they packed up, took care of the campsite and were on their way.

As if in answer to her prayer, she saw something that looked to her like smoke ahead. She called out, "Josh, is that smoke I see ahead of us? Have we found a settlement?"

He called back. "No, that is steam. I think we might be able to get you that bath. Let's go look."

They came to a pool of water fed by a spring of very warm water. Josh put his hand in the pool and told her, "Your bath awaits you, Madam," as he bowed like a butler.

Mary told him, "Why don't you go off into the forest and do whatever you do to find us some lunch while I take my bath?"

21

He began removing his clothes and told her, "Lunch is growing right beside this pond, and you are not the only one who is dirty. I'm going to take a bath, too." He was in his underwear and dove into the pool before she could think of a response. When he came up to the surface, he told her, "I have already seen you so you should have no compunction about your nudity now. The time for modesty has passed if you want to be clean."

She thought it over for a minute and decided he was right. He had seen her breasts, and she would be wearing her panties. She stripped down and dove in. They swam around for a few minutes, getting into a water fight, splashing each other and laughing. Eventually Josh went close to shore and began scrubbing his body with sand from the shoreline.

He told her, "This will work as well as soap to get you really clean, but don't rub too hard or you will have a rash." She came over close to him and began using the sand. Josh glanced down and noticed that her white panties had become transparent. Her red bush was as plain as day to his hungry eyes. He suddenly dove deep into the pond and tread water until his erection went down enough not to be obvious.

He climbed out of the pool and quickly got into his clothes, still wet. He told her, "I'll start preparing lunch while you finish." He stood behind the bushes picking raspberries as he watched her come out of the pool, take off her panties, dry herself with a shirt, put on dry panties and get dressed. He had his cap half full of berries when she finished. He had a problem with an erection that threatened to burst though his jeans. Hard concentration and her being covered helped. He finished filling the hat and brought their lunch over to where she was sitting, combing her hair.

She asked, "I wonder why this water is warm, and the stream is so very cold? What made it warm, and where does it get its heat?"

Josh was not about to tell her it was simply a warm spring, and there were probably a lot of them in the mountains. He went into more detail with a little elaboration thrown in. "This is fairly new country, geologically speaking. Most of these mountains are dormant volcanoes. They are filled with molten lava. There is a spring under the mountain from the snow on top melting and seeping into the ground. Lava from the mountain heats that water to the boiling point, and it rises up to the surface of the ground. By the time it reaches the air, it has usually cooled quite a bit. Over time, erosion from the water and elements created your bath for you."

She responded, "Molten lava? Do you mean to tell me we are on the side of a volcano?"

He answered, "Yes, it is a volcano, and yes, volcanoes do erupt now and then." He let her imagination take over. After the meal, she insisted that they move on right away. She did not want to be near that particular mountain any longer than she had to be.

Since the way they were going was downstream, most of their travel was downhill. Undergrowth was not a problem except near the stream. Josh went over to a particular willow and looked it over carefully before cutting off a large branch.

He continued along ahead of Mary, whittling away at the willow stick. He trimmed off all of the small branches, putting a half-dozen of the larger ones under his belt at his back. She could hear him humming an old Irish lullaby. It was one of her favorites so she began to sing. Her voice sounded as though the sky had opened, and an angel had come down to sing. At least that is what Josh felt as he listened. His heart seemed to keep up with the beat of the melody.

His realization that this lovely woman, with such a marvelous singing voice, could never be his, made him sad. He quickened his pace and widened the distance between them. She could not see him, but she followed the trail of pieces of bark and shavings he left behind. It was a full hour before she caught up to him. He was sitting on a log at the edge of a clearing, still working on the stick. He told her, "We will camp here. You prepare our camp, and I'll see what I can find to eat."

It was the first time he had ever given her orders and the first time she was asked to prepare the camp. Her temper began to flare up, but he never noticed. His back was toward her, and he was walking into the forest. He was back an hour later with two rabbits he had killed with the slingshot, one with his knife when the slingshot broke. He had to chuckle to himself. His secret was that he never needed the slingshot in the first place. It was just an excuse to get her out of that ridiculous bra. It was practical as well as being nice to see. The restriction on her chest of the tight garment affected her breathing so that she would run out of breath sooner. He wondered if she noticed that she was not as tired after a day's travel as she had first been.

It was also very nice to see her nipples poking the material of her shirt out and the movement of her breasts as she walked. He may not ever have her, but he determined that he would enjoy as much of her as his own personal code would allow.

She was quiet as they cooked the meal. She thought it wise to give him his space and let him sort out whatever was troubling him. She knew she had something to do with it and was worried that he was tiring of the whole ordeal and having her along was burdensome. Up to this point, she had been of little help and left everything up to him. The fact that she was a novice in the environment was not a good excuse. She could have learned and tried harder.

CHAPTER 6

The meal was almost ready when he said, "I guess I lost my job today."

She was confused and asked, "What do you mean? Do you mean your job of helping me get out of these mountains?"

"No, of course not," he replied. "I lost my teaching job today. This is the day of the beginning of the school year, and I am not there so they will replace me. I lost my job, but I don't feel bad about it. I can get another if they do not take me back. That is, if I want to work."

Mary decided, wrongly, that losing his job was what was bothering him. They talked little while eating, and since it was late, they turned in for the night. The ground felt harder to Mary. She realized that he had not dug up the dirt and loosened the soil. Then she knew why he had done all the digging. It was for her comfort. She reached up and opened the buttons of her shirt. She felt she needed to reward him and drop him a hint at the same time.

Mary felt his arm go around her and felt it rise just as it did every night. There was a hesitation when he discovered that her shirt was open, but he continued up until his hand was cupping her naked breast. Mary feigned sleep, but she felt her nipple harden and press into the palm of his hand. She could not stop her breathing from becoming faster, nor could she stop the moisture at her junction. She felt his hardened member press into her buttocks as well. It made her feel good that she affected him in that way. She thought, "Maybe, just maybe..."

He felt her naked breast and the hardened nipple and smiled. "Maybe, just maybe..." He lay still, engrossed in his own thoughts of just how much he wanted her. He went over his motives and knew it was not lust as much as it was love. That was what kept him from pushing her to have sex with him.

Mary had a difficult time dropping off to sleep. She remembered the sudden tingle as she entered the airplane and saw Josh. She was thrilled when she found herself seated next to him. When the plane crashed and they were the only survivors, she was frightened and was sure she would die. Josh led her off that horrid mountain and obviously saved her life.

She was beginning to actually enjoy their trek though the mountains and forest. This very day for the first time they had laughed together as they played in the water. He hummed as she sang, and she thought they sounded good together. She knew she was in love with Josh but was sure he would never have her since they were from different worlds, as she worked in big business and he taught school. She pictured his teaching children. She thought probably grade school. He seemed to have the patience to teach children that young.

During the night something happened in her attitude and her willingness to participate. When she awoke, she saw Josh preparing breakfast. She went over and gave him what assistance he would let her render. She was cheerful and gave him a hug and a kiss on the cheek as a morning greeting. She pitched in and helped break camp when it became time to get on the trail.

Josh liked the new Mary and hoped she would continue in the same mood and attitude. He also liked very much the fact that she had opened her shirt for him. He noticed that today her shirt was not buttoned all the way up, like she usually wore it. He could see her cleavage much more readily, and her breasts seemed to wiggle under their covering much more. He noticed a spring in her step that was not there before. She smiled more readily and was cheerful. He heard no complaints from her, and she never questioned his decisions about the trail. Up until now when they had walked, she had always followed him as though she was being led. This day she walked beside him whenever it was possible. All of this gave Josh the feeling that they were together instead of just a man leading a woman out of a bad situation. There was companionship that had never been present before, and it felt good.

He was satisfied that she was becoming a survivor instead of a victim. She was now hiking out and had learned to let him show her the ways of the wilderness. It had taken a while, but she was now a fellow traveler.

Josh carried the branch he had been whittling on, but had the smaller ones he saved tied to the duffle. It was taking the shape he wanted, and he knew they would have to stop for the night early so he would have time to finish the bow he had carved.

The canyon they were following to lower land narrowed on both sides, squeezing in toward the stream. Josh was concerned but said nothing. They heard the waterfall before they saw it. The stream just seemed to disappear as it tumbled over a cliff. There was only a narrow slippery ledge along one side that allowed Josh to ease along carefully and look over the falls to see how far the drop was. He quickly determined that there was no choice; they would have to go over the falls. High cliffs on both sides prevented them from going around, and the drop was only about 20 feet. He could see by the blue of the water that there was a deep pond at the bottom of the falls.

He asked her if she could swim. She wanted to know why, so he told her, "We have to jump about 20 feet down into a deep pond if we want to proceed." She told him, "I will follow you, Josh."

The way she said it was more of a commitment than an arrangement. There was something more than the present situation in that statement. Josh tried to heave the duffel over and onto the bank of the pond down below. It landed short and hit the water. It slowly began to drift, so he told her to wait until he waved her down, and he jumped off. He swam out of the pond and then ran downstream to retrieve the duffel before they lost it completely. He came back and immediately started to construct a large fire. He called up to her and beckoned her to jump, once the fire began to build.

He opened and emptied the duffel bag to discover that some of the contents were not very wet. He hung up a pair of jeans for her and one for himself. As she was swimming out of the pond, he was stripping down and getting into the drier jeans. Mary was initially shocked but enjoyed the view. She noted that Josh was not wearing underwear.

She felt the cold water and saw the dry jeans he had set out for her. Without further hesitation, she stripped completely and pulled the drier clothing up her shapely legs. Josh watched and could not help but get an erection. Mary noticed but said nothing. She was pleased that her body would create that response from him. A little smile parted her lips.

Mary said, "Well, nothing like a vigorous swim in cold water to wake up a person. I appreciate this fire a lot. Thank you."

Josh told her, "I thought you would enjoy it, and I know I do. Sorry everything else got wet so we will have to dry them out." Josh was able, with great difficulty, not to overtly stare at her very large breasts and protruding nipples.

When she noticed him looking, in spite of his efforts not to be caught, she said nothing and did not try to cover herself. She felt a strong stirring of her own, and her nipples hardened even more. They stood out as never before. She could not, and would not, blame Josh if his reactions were the same.

She wanted him to make love to her without delay. She had little experience with the opposite sex and so had no idea how to seduce a man. In actual fact she had never in her life had an intimate relationship.

Josh took off his jeans and dove into the pool. When he came up for air, he threw a large fish up onto the bank.

He told her, "I thought we might as well eat since we are going to be here a while." He stood by the fire until his body dried before he got back into his pants. The cold, cold water had taken care of his erection.

A milestone had been reached. They had been nude together, each knowing fully that the other was observing. It did not quash the feelings they each felt in any way, but it did make them more comfortable together. They had no secrets any more, at least as far as their bodies were concerned.

When everything dried, they packed the bag, cleaned up the camp and went on their way. It was pleasant by the waterfall, but they were no longer used to the noise made by the falls. They wanted to get back to where it was quiet.

That evening they camped a little early. Josh went out and brought back roots he had found, onions again, and berries he had picked. He also brought back a fresh beaver pelt and a large flat piece of meat.

Mary asked, "Is that the fur and some of the meat from one of those 'lumberjacks' like we saw earlier?"

He told her, "No, this is one of the delicacies of the forest. It is beaver tail, and this is the pelt of a beaver. I think it will come in handy. You will love the beaver tail. It tastes like chicken."

Under his watchful eye, she did the cooking and did a fine job. She used leaves and mud, just as Josh showed her, to cook the vegetables and meat in the hot coals of the fire.

Josh was busy by the stream picking up handfuls of sand and rubbing the wood on his new bow. He was polishing it. Afterward he passed it back and forth over the fire. Each time he got it warm, he would flex it so it would keep its strength and flexibility, not turn brittle and break.

He used the straight branches he had saved to make three arrows. The only thing he needed was an arrowhead for each and some feathers for stabilization.

He gained his feathers in an unusual way. Mary went off away from camp to where Josh had set up his makeshift outhouse with the toilet seat to take care of the call of nature. While she was gone, Josh reclined on their blankets and watched two birds high up in the air. It looked as though an eagle and a hawk were having a fight. They dove at each other repeatedly with claws and beaks. The fight did not last long. The birds flew off in separate directions. When Mary returned, she had two big feathers in her hand. She said they had just floated out of the sky and landed near her. She wanted to know what kind of bird had dropped the feathers. Josh looked and said, "bald eagle." He told her he needed at least one of the feathers, but she could wear one in her hair if she wanted.

He told her, "You are in the wilds; you could be a beautiful Indian Princess. The feather would only enhance that image."

She told him, "Thank you, sir," and curtsied. "If you need both feathers for your arrows, we should use them for that purpose. If you have some left over, maybe you could make more arrows. Use whatever is needed and store the leftovers for later use. I don't need any kind of jewelry out here."

He agreed, "No, you most certainly do not need any more decoration." She blushed.

Josh carefully split a feather along its shaft and fashioned his stabilizations. He glued them to the shaft with pitch from a pine tree and further secured them with the fishing line. All he needed then were arrowheads. He knew he would not have any anytime soon so he did the next best thing. He made a point at the end of each arrow, burned the point and cooled it several times. This hardened that part of the arrow. He was ready to go hunting with the bow and arrows.

A cold breeze blew through the trees, and Josh was concerned that winter was finally arriving. He knew it was early September and was actually surprised and happy that they had not seen snow since they came down from the top of the mountain.

By necessity they wore their clothes to bed. They helped keep them warm under the blanket. When they went to bed that night, she took her usual position with him spooned against her, but Josh turned his back so she was obliged to be the spoon, so to speak. Her breasts pushed against his back, just as his erection had been poking her for several nights previously. They were in bed for a while when she said, "You don't like me very much, do you?"

He was silent for an extended period of time. He felt her body jerk almost as though she was crying, but it was an emotional tear that formed in her heart, not her eyes. She was struggling not to cry when he said, "Yes, I like you. I like you more than you know."

CHAPTER 7

The tear in her heart turned from one of sorrow to one of joy. Mary was still thinking about what he said when she went to sleep. What did he mean when he said, "More than you know"?

They awoke to a cold, cold day. Josh told her to stay in bed until he got a good fire going and left her under the blanket. He brought in wood and built up a good-sized fire for her comfort. When he went to the creek, he noticed ice along the edges as he washed up.

As though the conversation had not ended several hours ago, she said, "How much is 'more than I know'?"

He looked at her a moment and thought it over before he said, "Are you sure you want to know?" She nodded. He told her, "I would like to tell you but not now, it might cause a big problem between us."

She stood up, her blouse wide open in the cold air. Her nipples were standing straight out in all their glory as she put her hands on her hips and said, "Josh McDougal, you will tell me right now, or there will definitely be a problem between us. You love me, don't you?"

He only nodded his head. He started to say he could not help it. He was in love with her the second she sat beside him in the airplane. She gave him no chance. "Then why have you never even kissed me? I welcomed your hand on my breasts and even opened my shirt for you. Yet you have not even attempted to kiss me. I felt your erection every night and knew you wanted to make love, but you did nothing. What is wrong? Is my body repulsive?"

She would have continued the tirade, but Josh's lips stopped it. He held her tight and told her, "I have loved you from the moment I saw you for the first time. I did not want to take advantage of our situation."

She told him, "Now I know why my heart skipped a beat when I saw who my seat partner was." They kissed again

31

tenderly and for a long time before they broke it off. She began to feel the cold and shivered. He told her to get dressed and to put on double everything before she froze to death.

They ate leftover meat and some berries they picked for breakfast and broke camp. Josh was thinking he would have to find a hide large enough to give them warmth at night. He considered beaver pelts sewn together and decided that would be the way he would provide for her comfort.

Later in the day they removed a layer of clothes because of the warmth. Josh was ahead on a narrow trail when he saw the antlers of a bull moose ahead, coming toward them. He motioned for her to get off the trail and fade into the brush. He came back and stood beside her as the giant beast passed. He looked at them and snorted, but otherwise was undisturbed by their presence until Mary slapped a mosquito that was on her neck.

The moose snorted, pawed the ground, lowered his massive horns and charged. Josh pulled Mary as he ran into the thickest patch of woods he could find. The moose missed his first charge, but saw them running and charged again. They made it into the trees, and the moose crashed into them with force. A couple of the smaller trees fell to the ground while others did not. His horns became hung up in some of the branches and saplings that had bent with the force and snapped back into place. Josh led Mary out onto their original path and ran until he felt Mary could not run another step.

As they rested, Josh kept an eye out for the enraged bull moose. Mary asked, "Why did he do that? He seemed determined to kill us. I don't understand."

Josh told her, "It is rutting season. It is time when a bull moose will charge anything unusual and many things that are ordinary. It lasts about a month and drives the normally docile animal crazy. He was not mad at us; he was just mad."

Mary thought she probably knew what "rutting season" meant and kept quiet.

They came across another beaver dam and watched from a distance while the animals worked. Two were nearby cutting down saplings while a third busied itself dragging branches into the dam. They were building, or reinforcing, their winter home - a mud and stick construction in the water which they could enter and sleep in, have babies, and whatever. Reluctantly, Josh used all three of his arrows to dispatch the three beavers. They would be blankets for the two travelers. When he recovered his arrows, only one was no longer useful.

It was the first time Mary had ever witnessed Josh killing an animal. He went to each of the three animals and was saying something to each. It sounded as though he might be praying. She asked him about it as he cleaned the kill and skinned them out.

He told her, "After the fashion of my ancestors on my mother's side, I was thanking the Great Spirit and them for giving us their lives. Because of their sacrifice we shall be comfortable and we shall live. We owed them thanks."

They made camp early so he could scrape the hides from any remaining meat or other matter. Mary roasted the three beavertails over the fire. They would pack along the excess cooked meat for consumption later.

Josh constructed a rack downwind from their campfire. He cut large strips of meat from the beavers and put it on the rack. The heat from the fire would dry the meat, and the smoke would keep flies away, plus give the meat flavor. She asked him why, of course. He told her, "It is an old Indian way of preserving food for later use. It is called jerky. This will have somewhat of a smoky flavor, but you will probably like it."

She said, "Please don't tell me it will taste like chicken." The smile told him she was onto his little joke.

After getting the hides clean, Josh placed them fur side down on a large flat rock. With another rock tied to a stick he began beating the hides all over. Mary asked if she could help. She joined him in beating the hides after he made her a hammer of her own. He explained that it was to tenderize the hides and make them more flexible. He told her it was not tanning them, but was the next best thing.

It was nearly dark when Josh decided they had to call it

done. They ate, prepared their bed and laid both blankets down for protection from the cold ground. Each had two beaver pelts. One pelt to cover their legs and one for their upper body. There was some overlap so they were completely covered. He told her, "As long as we lay still, I think we will be warm enough. We will smell like beaver, but at least we will be warm. Tomorrow I will sew them together."

The couple was warm, but they still cuddled together. They kissed and said good night. Out of habit they were wearing their clothes, but that did not stop them from opening buttons for their exploring hands. Neither one got much sleep. They talked of their love most of the night.

Josh finally was privileged to suck and kiss those fabulous mounds on her chest. She finally for the first time felt what a man's penis was like. It was all he could do to stop a climax. It was the first time in his life that he had ever been this intimate with a woman.

Morning and another snowfall came too early for the lovers. They broke camp and proceeded downstream. This time Mary carried the lighter load of the duffel, and Josh carried the heavy pelts. They ate leftover beaver tail as they walked.

They were only a half mile from their last camp when their stream joined a larger one. The one they followed had gotten larger as small streams joined it, but this one joining the other was the beginning of a river. It really was not a big river yet, but it was a great encouragement to them, and yet a disappointment in a way. They felt their journey was coming to an end. They had both began to enjoy the outing.

They went in a generally southern direction, and the new river continued on that course. They continued downstream, confident that they would find some kind of civilization. The airplane was off course, and they had no idea where the crash happened. They did not know that there was still a long, long trek ahead of them.

Josh looked back up the trail to fix the location in his mind as he had done many times. He would need the information eventually. What he first saw were ominous storm clouds coming toward them. He knew the first big blizzard of the season would hit them before nightfall.

He told her, "Mary, there is a storm coming; we have to find very good shelter in a hurry. Keep your eyes open for a cave. That would be our best bet." Their pace quickened to nearly a trot. They checked out three likely spots that would never do before they came to one that he knew would be deep enough and had a small opening. There were the hairs of a bear clinging to one of the rocks at the entrance, and he saw bear tracks entering.

He told her, "Wait here and don't make a sound. I have to look to see if there is a vacancy in this domicile." She gave him a strange look but said nothing. With great caution Josh quietly entered the cave. He knew they had to take the shelter. He lit one of his lighters and saw what he expected. A young boar bear was fast asleep not far inside. He saw no other sign of occupants.

He notched one of his arrows and approached the animal. He took the risk of lighting the lighter again to aim his shot accurately to the place just behind the front leg. He pulled the bow as far as he could stretch the bowstring and fired. Quickly he notched and fired the second arrow. One of them hit a rib and broke, but the other went between ribs and lodged in the bear's heart. Josh didn't see it because he had already left the cave.

Mortally wounded, the bear got up and stumbled out of the cave. Josh was there waiting for him. He jumped on the bear's back, reached around with the Bowie and slit the bear's throat.

Mary gathered wood after putting the duffel bag and beaver pelts in the cave. Josh expertly skinned his kill, quartered it and had the quarters hanging from tree limbs. He was helping Mary bring in one more armload of wood when the storm hit.

They built a fire close to the opening to the cave. This served three purposes. It would keep predators such as other bears or mountain lions away. It would heat the cave and form a barrier of heat to keep the cold out. Finally, it would allow the smoke from the fire to escape without filling the cave.

Josh busied himself preparing the bear's hide in the same manner as he did the beaver pelts. When he was satisfied, he cut off the leg fur and constructed two small bags. He sewed the beaver pelts together and shaped them more or less into a square. He put the excess fur from the legs and neck into the two bags. In the end he had two stuffed bags they could use for pillows.

Mary, of course, cooked some of the bear meat for dinner and helped Josh in the "tenderizing" of the bear hide. They had a good laugh when Mary remarked, "Mum, this tastes just like chicken."

The floor of the cave was covered in sand and dirt blown in over the years and was very loose. Josh found a good spot for their bed, laid down the bear hide fur side up and then covered it with the blankets. The beaver pelt "blanket"covered everything. He placed their new pillows at the head of the bed.

They sat close together for a long time listening to the storm howl outside. They never said much, just held each other, lost in their own thoughts and occasionally kissing tenderly. He finally said, "It's like we have slipped back in time, and we have become cave dwellers. I have to say I like our private cave."

She kissed his lips and said, "As long as you are my caveman, I like it too."

"Well, then," he said, "If I am your caveman, does that mean I have to hit you over the head with a club and drag you by the hair over to the bed?"

CHAPTER 8

She looked at him and told him, "I know what we intend to do in that bed tonight, and I want to do it as much as you. However, there is something I have to tell you first while there is still time. Once we are in that bed, everything will just fly out of my head. I want you so much it hurts.

"Josh, I am a virgin, a 24-year-old virgin. I have never had a man become more intimate with me than you have been. I know nothing about making love and am worried that I will disappoint you as a lover."

His reply surprised her, "Well, my love. I want so much to make love to you and look forward to tonight with great anticipation, but we are actually on equal footing here. I have never made love to a woman in my life. The first pussy I ever even saw, other than in pictures, was yours. I have never held a breast or sucked one before, only yours. I guess you will not disappoint me or me you because neither of us knows what to expect of the other. I think we will learn together how to please one another. I guess you would call me a 28-year-old virgin."

It started to get dark outside, and the fire had died down somewhat. Josh told her they did not need much of a fire and put the two largest pieces of wood on the fire. It would burn between the two but consume the wood slowly. They went over to the bed. Mary was going to just get between the covers with her clothes on as usual when Josh began to undress. She followed suit.

They watched each other as they slowly exposed their bodies. When he exposed his chest, she exposed hers and so on until the hot sensuous "dance" had them totally naked. They had seen each other naked before, but this time there was electricity in the air. They were disrobing for a different and exciting reason.

Josh took their clothes and put them under the covers at the foot of the bed. "So they will be warm in the morning when we put them on." She got into the bed and pulled his side down so he could get in. He stood and watched as she sat up and held out her arms to welcome him to their consummation bed. Josh was in bed and in her arms before she had them fully raised.

They knew they would undoubtedly be unable to travel for at least a day or two, and they had all the time in the world for their first experience of physical love. They kissed and kissed, tongues dancing together as their passion built. He fondled her breasts as he kissed her ears and neck. He was lightly fondling her nipple between his thumb and forefinger when he got to her throat and upper chest. Eventually he sucked on one of her nipples as he pulled and squeezed the other. He treated each mound the same over and over. She trembled, and her hips rose off the bed as a climax took over.

In the meantime, she ran her hands over his chest and finally reached his manhood. She held it for a long time before she started moving her hand up and down slowly. He reached down and put his hand on her mound. He rose up and looked her square in the eyes with a serious expression on his face. He said, "This is forever if we continue."

She kissed him deeply and told him, "Yes, darling, yes, this is forever."

He made love to her then. For a long time he went slowly and tenderly, afraid he would hurt her, but eventually their passion overtook them. She reached her peak and went over; he was with her all the way. For the rest of the night, they made love through the valleys and over the peaks time and again. In the wee hours of the morning they fell asleep exhausted and still joined.

Late in the day they awoke and made love again before starting their day, knowing that they were now man and wife. There was no paperwork yet, but the emotional and spiritual bonds were there.

CHAPTER 9

Josh got out of bed and stirred the hot coals while adding very small sticks. He blew on the coals until a flame started and then added wood. When the cave was warm, he woke up his dozing bride with kisses.

Breakfast consisted of bear steaks Mary roasted over the fire. As the meat was cooking, they decided to look out to see how much snow had fallen and how much time it would take before they could move further down river. They were not surprised to see deep snow and a grey sky.

She smiled and took him by the hand, leading him back to their bed. The meat was well-cooked when they finally ate.

Josh began looking around inside the cave and noticed that it was not a cave at all but an old mine. The front portion was rather large for a mine, and it had fooled him at first, but the tunnel that led off toward the heart of the mountain was definitely a mine.

The snow outside was giving way to warmer weather after another day. He was taking a look when his foot stepped on a metal object which turned out to be an old pick. He could see the marks of a pick, maybe that same one, on the walls. He saw one or two flakes of gold so concluded that it had been a gold mine that had probably played out.

He told Mary and then concluded that if there were a mine, there might be a miner's cabin fairly close. It might yield some necessities or maybe even shelter for the winter. He knew there was no way they were going to be able to travel before long, and he needed time to gather provisions. He told his new bride as much. She agreed that the best thing to do would be to hole up until spring. She told him she didn't care if they never left the mountains.

He told her, "That would not be fair to our son."

She looked bewildered and said, "You made me pregnant with a son? I wonder, was it the first time we made love?"

He told her, "Yes, it was the first time. That is one of the reasons I told you that this is forever. You just wait nine months and see. Until then, you are not traveling much, and I will take care of you. I know what to do from advanced first aid classes."

It was about noon three days later before they left the old mine. They had traveled nearly a mile before Josh spotted an old cabin in a clearing that had been nearly taken back to nature by brush and bushes. It was only about a dozen feet square. Some of the roof was missing, and the old door hung askew. There were no windows in the cabin, and it looked solid enough.

Inside they found a dust-covered treasure trove. There was a cook stove that would also heat the place, as well as pots and pans, along with silverware and cookware. The old cot was just under the missing part of the roof so the bedding and mattress were gone as well as the wooden bed. The bed, the table, and one lonely chair were all no better than firewood. If they meant to stay, Josh had his work cut out for him.

Mary found what was left of an old broom and began sweeping the place out. She had made the decision. Josh went out to see what there was around the place to replace some roof. He found no lumber, of course, so he took the axe, which was surprisingly sharp for its age, and went into the woods.

He cut pine branches and carried them back, making several trips. He pulled up large clumps of dry grass and piled them up beside the house. He built a grid of sticks over the empty space where the roof was missing. Then he placed the grass on the roof one tier at a time until the whole roof was covered not once but several times. The pine branches went on next, and then he repeatedly covered the roof several times. Most of his fishing line was used to tie things down so the wind could not easily blow everything off onto the ground. That would keep out the snow and rain for at least a year and also provide insulation on the roof.

In the meantime, Mary had done an amazing job of cleaning their house and starting a fire. Josh did not even see her when she went to the river for water. When he came into the house, she had water boiling and meat in the pot. Josh told her, "Wait a minute. I have a surprise for you."

He went out again and a few minutes later came in with a few potatoes about the size of his fist. He said, "The old miner must have had a garden out back. There are vegetables growing out there. I'll harvest them. We will dry them out on the warm side of the stovetop and use them for soup stock. All we will need is meat. I will go back and get the rest of the bear tomorrow."

She told him, "You are not the only one with a surprise." She took an old kerosene lamp off a shelf and set it on the floor. She told him she found a full two- gallon can of kerosene under the shelves where she was cleaning. Josh lit the lamp, and they had light by which to eat and to set up their bedroll. While the meal finished cooking, Josh went to work on the door and got it to work by using a piece of old leather as hinges. They were ready for their first night.

Mary went outside and told Josh he had to carry her over the threshold. They entered their winter home kissing with her in his very willing arms. They made love once and went to sleep.

The next morning she started breakfast using potatoes fried in bear grease and fried bear steaks. Josh hurried back to the mine and collected two quarters of bear meat while she cooked. He had worked up a good appetite for breakfast and said he had never eaten such a delicious meal. He went back and got the rest of the meat before starting on his next project.

He cut a great many of the branches from the bushes and even in many cases the bush itself. From these he made chairs, using the main stock of the bush for legs and weaving the branches together. He needed leather for binding it all together. The nylon fish line would stretch over time, so he needed something that would shrink from a wet to dry state and hold.

He went hunting and found a bull elk. He only had the one arrow, but he wounded the elk enough so he could kill it with his knife. This time the arrow was broken. He hung the elk by its horns up in a tree and dressed it out. The hide and one rear quarter he carried back to the cabin.

Mary had not been idle. She had rigged up a drying rack just as she had seen Josh do it and was drying bear meat outside the cabin when he came up with the elk and elk hide. He smiled at her resourcefulness and realized she had not let much slip past her along the way. She saw the hindquarter he was carrying and asked what it was.

He told her, "I got an elk. I will go back and get the rest of him soon. Nice job with the jerky project."

She looked at him and told him, "Don't tell me. It tastes like chicken. Just like the rabbit and the beaver and some of the other things you fed me on the trail."

He laughed and told her, "You are a wonder. How long did you believe me?"

She answered, "No further than the first bite of the first rabbit."

They kissed as they watched the meat turn into a winter's supply or at least part of the winter's supply. Josh made two trips back for the horns and the other quarters of the elk. He set to work immediately, dressing the elk hide and scraping off the hair. He wanted most of the hide to be rawhide so he could use it as a tabletop. He cut a long strip of green hide about 3/8 of an inch wide from the legs. These he used to tie together the parts of the chairs and to make a frame for the table. The hide was tightly spread over the frame to make a tabletop. He used nails he found in the cabin and the green strips to make sure it was good and tight. When everything dried out, it would be very sturdy.

Mary was once more amazed at his skill and once more realized there was much more to this man than she knew. Whatever it was, she loved and was grateful he had the skills. She knew in her mind that if any other man had survived the crash with her, they would both be dead. It was only a twist of fate or a blessing that Josh had been there to save her.

They carefully carried the table and the chairs into the house and set them down. They would not be able to use them for a couple of days until the hide dried and tightened. She served their dinner on the floor as they sat cross-legged and ate by lamp light. They were very tired from their day's work and went to sleep while still kissing and playing with each other's body.

The next morning Josh went out to harvest the vegetables. He brought in loads of carrots, peas, beans, and potatoes. The miner was a smart old dude. He planted beans that would furnish nourishment and would stay good for a long, long time. Josh fashioned a bag out of a pair of his jeans and filled the legs with shelled beans. He used a shirt to fill with peas that they had dried and mixed them with dried carrots. The drying process took several days. It took about an hour to dry a batch, and there were many batches.

He built a bin for potatoes that was high enough that Mary could barely reach into it to get some for their meals. He constructed the bin in such a way that the top layer of logs could be removed and used for firewood as the bin of potatoes got used up. Short pine blocks were notched and set one on another to form a rectangular box. Each layer was a separate, yet integrated, part of the whole. As the level of contents went down, she simply removed that layer of blocks.

They found that the brush was mostly blueberries and huckleberries. Some of the fruit had not fallen or been eaten, so they gathered all they could find and put them in pots and pans. Their larder soon took up over half of the small cabin.

Their biggest problem was storage places. The duffel was emptied of clothes and filled. Josh's spare pants and spare shirt, along with the spare pants and shirt belonging to Mary, were used. They ran out of things to fill with their winter food. Everything that could hold something was used. Josh had to bring in more game, if for no other reason than their hides.

The next big chore was to make more arrows. Josh found a willow that grew very straight and was very hard wood once dried. Over time he fashioned arrows by the dozens. Here and there he found a feather some bird had lost so he kept them for stabilization feathers. He tried the first one out on another elk and found it flew straight and true. The elk hide was used to make them a bed and the meat dried into jerky.

He lashed together a bedstead with sturdy pine and covered

it with the green hide. When it dried, it was as sturdy as a rock. Also very heavy since all the poles he used were about four inches in diameter.

Two deer gave them more variety of meat and hides to make bags to replace pants and shirts. Horns were used for clothes hangers and pegs for bags of food. Two more deer finally gave them all the storage they needed and a lot more meat in the form of jerky than they needed.

Mary helped in every way and even began to learn to use the bow and arrow. One of the deer was her kill. Josh was pleased that she learned so fast and so well. She was a genuine "pioneer wife."

They brought wood from the deadfall in the forest and from along the riverbank. Josh cut and stacked it along the walls of the cabin on the outside. They had wood stacked three layers thick on all sides except the doorway. They were prepared for winter with one exception.

Josh went downstream from the house a little ways and dug a hole. Above the hole he constructed an outhouse out of pine poles, notched and set on one another. He used pine boughs for the roof. It was solid and sturdy. He installed the airplane toilet seat. They were then prepared for winter's storms.

It had been just over a month, and yet the weather held off as though waiting for them to get ready. The day Josh finished the outhouse it began to snow. By morning there was a foot of snow on the ground.

CHAPTER 10

They began their hibernation by making love. It seemed to snow nearly every day, and every day Josh broke a trail to the outhouse. He brought in wood for the fire and went to the river for water when they needed it. They took sponge bathes every day or two for cleanliness; as a rule they bathed each other. That ritual always led them back to the bed for some reason.

Knowing that he would need snowshoes before winter ended, Josh found some limber branches and bent them into a teardrop shape. He tied the ends together, and then meticulously wove leather strips to cover each snowshoe. He had thongs to tie them to his boots.

Eventually the river was completely frozen over but dangerous because going out on that ice could be fatal if it broke under your feet. They used snow water by melting snow from right outside their door.

The months passed, and Mary began to show the growth of a fetus within her womb. Josh told her the baby would come in mid-June. He began doing much more of the work inside and all of the outside chores. She discovered that Josh was a fine cook and a fine housekeeper. She helped as much as he would let her.

It was not really a harsh winter for that part of the world. The snow accumulated only about three feet, but that didn't stop the wolves from being hungry. Each night they could hear the howls. It seemed they ranged closer and closer to the cabin. Mary was frightened, but Josh comforted her and told her the stories about wolves attacking humans were greatly exaggerated.

"The stories one reads about wolf packs harassing some poor stranded trapper or traveler are all just to tell a story. They are pure fiction. There are no recorded incidents of a wolf or a wolf pack attacking humans. There are incidents of a rabid wolf attacking, but that has nothing to do with hunger or even food." He did not tell her that a very hungry predator animal would do anything for food.

Grizzly bears were introduced to Mary in a unique way. It

happened during the day. There was a bang on their door and noises outside. Josh got up from the bed and looked out. A deer had stumbled through the deep snow and into the door while trying to escape the jaws of a bear.

The grizzly was close to within ten feet of his prey when Josh put an arrow through one eye. He stopped just long enough for a second arrow to put out his other eye. Josh began putting arrows into the animal as fast as he could aim and release. In the end there were four arrows penetrating the grizzly bear's heart, two in his eyes, and one that went through his neck. Josh left the bear lying on the ground until the deer calmed down. After about an hour, he shot and killed the deer.

It took a lot of work to dress out the animals in the deep snow. He had to carry the entrails out away from the cabin so the wolves could eat them. They thought they would not need all of the meat so he only took the hindquarters of the two animals, some of the fat from the bear for cooking grease, and the two hides. The rest was carried out and placed near the forest.

Mary asked why he had waited to kill the deer. He told her, "Adrenalin will make meat taste bad, and that deer was full of it with that bear chasing it. I thought it best to let the animal calm down."

That night they listened to the snarls and fighting among the wolves as they divided their meal in their own fashion. It was two days before they heard the howls again. This time they were much closer.

Each night and frequently during the day, Mary felt the need for Josh to comfort her. They wound up making love several times a day. Her pregnancy seemed to trigger anxieties and also made her very horny. She could not seem to get enough loving, both physically and emotionally. Of course, Josh did not mind that little quirk in the least.

The bear hide gave them more comfort for their bed. They put it down under their blankets so the bed would be softer. There were more bags for storage because of the deer, which did seem to make a little more room in their tight quarters.

With little to do on a daily basis, they spent a lot of their time in bed cuddled together. They experimented with various positions and variations of making love. Their experience was lacking, but they had accumulated knowledge of how men and woman had sex and the various varieties of the act.

They discovered that they both loved to satisfy the other orally. She liked his taste and he loved hers. This, of course, was a good thing because eventually they would not be able to have sex the normal way at all. For some period of time it would not be wise to use the "missionary" position so they experimented and found that she enjoyed having him enter her from behind while she lay on her side.

They did what they could around the house together, but it was so crowded that one could do as much as two since they got in each other's way. They began to take turns. Mary came up with the cravings associated with pregnancy, but there was little they could do about them. Pickles were hard to come by way out there in the woods. They laughed about that.

Their usual meal was stew made from jerky, dried vegetables, and potatoes with beans thrown in. The stew pot was always on, and they ate whenever they were hungry. They paid no attention to time at all. The cabin was dark most of the time because they were conserving fuel for the lamp. The two-gallon can of kerosene Mary found that first day would not last forever.

Josh figured it was about Christmas time. He thought long and hard before he came up with an idea. He boiled some of the dried berries and later mixed them with snow to make a "kind of, sort of, ice cream." She was thrilled and wanted more of the concoction. Josh made more for her until she was satisfied.

For Christmas dinner Josh served a roast he cooked on top of the stove. It was the last of the fresh venison. They celebrated Christmas, but the only gifts exchanged were themselves. They exchanged gifts many times that day. At least they thought it was Christmas. Josh was sure of the month and knew it was within a day or two.

Almost every night they talked about their baby and teased

about if it would be a boy or girl. Josh never wavered on his statement that the baby was a son. They talked about how handsome he would be and how he would look. They planned their future, never further than living in the woods. She even mentioned that he would have to make their cabin a lot larger for next winter.

She said they would need a storage room, nursery, living room with kitchen in it and a bedroom. They planned their house there where they lived.

Josh mentioned that they were on their honeymoon and eventually would have to return to civilization. She agreed it was the longest honeymoon on record and wanted it to continue forever. He promised it would do just that if he had anything to do with it.

Mary told about her childhood and growing up in the corporate world. She talked about all of her trials and tribulations as well as her joys and happiness. He let her ramble on for hours.

Josh was quiet about his own childhood and background. It was not an interesting subject to him. She was curious but did not want to open any complex issues, so to speak. She knew she loved the man he was, and that was enough for her.

CHAPTER 11

They were too much in love for cabin fever to cause a problem. As time passed, Josh used Mary's stomach as a sort of calendar. As she grew in size, he marked off the months in his mind. He could easily read the stars and tell you the approximate time and day of the year, but reading Mary's progress was a lot more fun. They were thrilled when the baby kicked for the first time. From that time on, Josh felt her stomach frequently. Josh used bear grease as a lotion to ease the stretching of her stomach just as Indians used in bygone days.

Early in the year, they had forgone clothing unless they had a need to go outside where it was cold. It was much more handy to be naked together and a lot more sensuous. To Mary's delight it provoked a lot more lovemaking.

They were in bed making love when Josh noticed a change in the wind outside of the cabin. They had listened to many blizzards and storms, but this one was different in tone from the others. Josh smiled to himself. While they were cuddling, Josh told her, "I think I have a surprise for you in the morning."

She could not get him to tell her any more. She went to sleep wondering what her man had on his mind. When she woke up the next day, Josh was already up and the door was wide open. He was cooking breakfast wearing no clothes, but seemed perfectly comfortable even though the door normally let in mass amounts of cold air. She got up and went to the door. She felt a warm wind against her skin and saw that most of the snow was gone. Nearly three feet of snow had disappeared overnight.

She asked, "What is it? What happened to the snow? How did you know?"

Josh told her, "I noticed a different tone to the wind and knew it had switched direction to come from the south. That usually means a Chinook wind. A Chinook is merely a warm wind. They usually come in about February, and this is February. I know because you are five months along."

49

She hit his shoulder with her hand and said, "You couldn't know it is February just from that."

He told her, "Well, to tell the truth, I did go out early before the sun took away the night and read the stars. They confirmed that it was February."

She answered him, "How do the stars tell you things like that? I didn't know that could be done."

"Well", he said, "there it was right up there in the sky. The word was spelled out by the stars for all to see." He waved his arm as though spelling and spoke each letter, moving his hand as though pointing to it, F E B R U A R Y." She laughed but wondered how he actually knew.

Just then the baby kicked. She said, "See that? Not even Little Josh believes your malarkey."

"No. My son is telling you that you should believe my malarkey. He is sticking up for his daddy."

Mary was convinced it was a boy. No young lady would kick her so very much. Sometimes she felt him kick on both the left and right sides at the same time. He would be an active boy.

The river was a raging torrent. It had risen to overflowing and even flooded an area close to the cabin. Mary could understand why the miner had built on higher ground. The noise made by the river was disturbing to her at first, but she was fascinated. They put on some clothes and walked out to the riverbank. They watched as trees floated down stream and listened as boulders rolled down the riverbed under the water. The water was filled with dirt and debris.

Josh told her, "I think this thaw was quick and through. It must have melted ice and snow way up high to cause this much water. I see big trees that have withstood spring floods for years going down river. I hope it doesn't get any higher. It could force us to vacate."

Downstream from them, the river widened and became shallower. This caused branches under water on the big trees to drag and hang up on the riverbed. They began to pile up into a logjam. The river was blocked by the big trees, and the smaller stuff began to fill in so as to cause a dam.

During the night the river water backed up and flooded most of the area where the cabin was located. Josh woke up and discovered over an inch of water on the floor. He jumped out of bed and began taking things off the floor so the water would not damage much of their larder.

He marked the doorjamb with a notch and kept vigilance to tell if the water was rising. After an hour, the notch was still at water level so he thought they were safe as far as being flooded out was concerned. He went back to bed and slept fitfully until daylight.

He checked his marker and found that the water was a good inch over his notch. He woke Mary, and they prepared to vacate to higher ground. Mary was in water over her knees in some areas as they made their way. Josh carried as much of their supplies as he could handle. He left Mary on dry ground and made trip after trip, emptying the cabin of everything he could move. He even carried out the chairs so they would have a comfortable place to sit. The bed was left behind, along with the table and, of course, the stove.

They set up a camp and waited beside their fire as they watched the water slowly rise. Toward evening they heard a tremendous roar as the logjam gave way under the pressure of water. By morning the river was much lower and running freely. The cabin was once again on what one would call dry ground. They made their way back and began the clean-up. Their cleaning and drying out the cabin took a full day. Josh cleaned out the stove and built a good fire in it to speed up the drying process. It took two days of hard work for them to get moved back in.

That night it snowed again before turning very cold. In the morning the river was down a lot, and there was a foot of snow on the ground. They went back to their routine of hibernation. It would be two months before they would see the sun again.

One night they were in the fiercest blizzard of the year. The winds were strong and cold. Sections of the roof blew away. Before long, the roof was as it had been when they first saw the cabin, minus a couple more boards. Snow blew in and covered their bed and the rest of the exposed part with four inches of snow. They could only wait until the blizzard blew itself out. There would be no going out into that storm.

The next morning the wind was calm, and they began the job of cleaning out the snow. Josh did most of the work and made sure Mary stayed in bed where it was warm. Eventually he removed the snow, and the fire he had going in the stove began to heat most of the house.

He went outside to survey the damage. He found most of the branches but none of the grass. He took two of their precious hides and patched the roof using the rest of the nails they had found when they moved in. They had to give up the bearskin cushion on their bed and consolidated some of the dried supplies to fix the roof. He heated some bear grease and covered the leather with it to prevent leaks. The bear grease would prevent water from absorbing into the leather and then dripping into the house.

Behind the can of nails, Josh discovered an old file. It was rusty, but it would work to sharpen the dull double bitted axe. At the first opportunity, he sat down and went to work on that vital tool.

Winter was not going to let go of the North Country easily. The storms were more frequent, and the winds were more powerful. Josh's new roof held. They spent three days with one blizzard blowing outside. Josh used a big kettle as a commode for Mary's use so she would not be obligated to leave the house. He emptied and cleaned it on a daily basis.

Wolves hung around the house outside. They were starving, so Josh would take great hands full of jerky from their larder and throw it out for them. Whatever they could spare they threw out to the animals. There were at least ten of them that used the cabin walls as shelter from the wind. They never bothered Josh when he went out to the privy and back or gathered snow for water. In fact, they usually ran off when he appeared.

He stepped out one day and heard a bark. It surprised him. Wolves do not bark; only a dog barks. That particular bark was right at the corner of the house. He looked to see a dog looking at him. On closer inspection he suspected it was a shepherd/husky mix. It was wild and ran off shortly.

Every time he went out, the dog would be there with the wolves. He would stay when the wolves ran and each day would come closer. Josh spent time talking to the animal and coaxing it. He would feed the dog by tossing him some jerky, each time a little closer so that eventually he only had to drop it on the ground.

One day he fed it by holding out a piece of jerky. Instead of snapping up the meat, the dog gently took it out of his hand and trotted off. For the next few days he fed the dog by hand.

One night they heard a scratching on the door and a whimper rather than a bark. Soon afterward he heard a low bark. He opened the door, and the dog walked in as though he owned the place.

He sniffed around, becoming familiar with his new surroundings. He approached Mary and sniffed her. To her embarrassment that sniffing was right between her legs. Josh told her that it was the way dogs have to know their friends. After a few minutes, he let both of them pet him for the first time.

Josh went back to bed thinking about how much havoc that dog could cause by being inside. Their supplies were not "dog proof." The dog made himself comfortable on the floor right beside the bed. He was on a fur Josh had laid down so Mary would not have to stand on the cold floor. In the morning the dog was still there when Josh stepped out of bed and almost on the dog. Josh opened the door, and the dog ran out; then he went back to bed.

An hour later the dog wanted back in again. He returned to his former position and seemed to sleep. Actually he watched every move Josh made as he stirred up the fire to warm the stew. Once the fire was established, Josh went back to bed to cuddle with Mary, who was now awake. The dog decided he needed some attention as well, so he got between them. They scratched him behind the ears and petted him until the stew was hot. He lay down on the floor between them as they sat down to eat. Once they were through, they designated a bowl as his and fed him.

Josh told Mary, "I would say we have been adopted. I wonder where he came from. He obviously has been wild and running with the wolves for a while, yet he seems trained. From the scars on his coat I would say he earned the right to be in the pack."

Mary was in the outhouse one day when the dog started barking and growling. Josh could see he was looking toward the outhouse. He saw what the dog was looking at. A cougar was lying on top of the outhouse looking at them. Josh got his bow and arrows and was ready in case the cat meant harm. When Mary stepped out of the door, the cougar looked her over and jumped off the back of the building, headed for the woods. She could not believe it when Josh told her what happened. "That dog alerted me to your danger. That cat could have pounced on you instead of running away."

A large Lobo wolf started hanging around. And the dog didn't like it. It was as though the wolf was trying to get the dog back into the pack. The two animals fought every now again just for a nip or two. The dog always went to the house when the older animal was around so their little squabbles did not happen often.

Finally one day they really got into it. There was fur flying and blood on both. Each one was trying for the other's throat, but neither could quite get a grip. Finally the old Lobo dove for the dog's throat, but instead of attacking as before, the dog backed up a bit. This extended the wolf's neck a little so the dog came in low and got a good grip. The Lobo was beat and knew it. The dog let him go and watched as he slowly retreated into the forest.

Mary was amazed that the dog had not killed the wolf. Josh told her, "Very few animals will kill the other in a fight. They don't lose their temper like humans. They kill to eat, not for any other reason. Of course there are exceptions."

A week later Josh felt that the weather was mild enough for him to go hunting for fresh meat. He left the house under an overcast but nonthreatening sky. It took him some time and distance before he found a deer that he promptly killed and hung by its horns to dress out.

While he worked, a wind came up and it began to snow. He hurried to finish, but the wind grew stronger, and the snow fell harder. He was in a whiteout by the time he put the deer carcass on his shoulders and started toward home. He could not see any landmarks because of the wind and snow.

He walked until the deer became too much for him. He dropped it and continued on in the direction he thought the cabin was. He did exit the forest and felt good about that. It should not be far to home. He kept moving although he was very tired. He had been very cold, but he began to feel warmer.

He knew that he was beginning to freeze to death, and to stop and rest meant certain death. He concentrated on making it home to his family.

He had been gone a long time, and Mary was worried, especially when the storm blew up. She waited anxiously for him to stumble through the door. Nothing happened.

In desperation she opened the door and told the dog, "Go find Josh, boy. Go find him." The dog looked at her and tipped his head to one side as she continued to plead with him. He trotted out the door.

Josh was about to give himself up to the elements when something jumped against him, almost knocking him to the ground. The dog barked and let Josh know he was there. He continued barking as he led Josh toward safety. Josh followed the sound of barking. Before long he saw in the whiteness of the snow a large dark object. The dog had led him home.

It took some time for Josh to warm up. Mary put him to bed right away and stirred up the fire. She fed him hot broth. The dog was right at his feet and refused to move while he slept for a full twelve hours. He suffered from chilblains in his hands for a week.

CHAPTER 12

April brought rain one day and snow the next. One day would be mild, and the next day it would turn cold. It was as though spring and winter were having a fight. Josh knew spring would win eventually, but winter just did not want to let go. One nice thing about it was that Josh brought in fresh game for food. He never did find the deer he had killed the day he almost froze. He thought the wolves must have eaten it and dragged off whatever remained.

Of course the river was high, filled with the spring run-off. As the weather became more consistently warm, the plants began to grow. While the soil was still damp, Josh went out and pulled a lot of grass from the area where the garden grew. It would give room for the plants he wanted. He used the shovel to loosen the soil. This allowed oxygen into the soil more readily.

As he dug around, he noticed the dog had come across an old metal box about four inches underground and nearly in the middle of where he figured the garden was originally planted. He thought the dog was after a mouse or something when he heard the dog's toenails scrape on metal. He dug it out and washed off the dirt in the river before bringing it into the house.

He and Mary pried open the lid, which was rusted shut, to discover the old miner's stash. There were four leather bags of gold nuggets. Josh told his wife that if they ever went back to civilization, it would give them a good start. One nugget was quite large, and Josh looked it over carefully. He had an idea.

Every day he spent a long time carving at that nugget, letting the flakes and shavings fall onto a piece of deer hide and saving them in the leather bags. The nugget began to take shape. Mary had an idea what he was doing and wisely kept quiet. He used every spare minute to carve away with the Bowie knife on that nugget. He eventually fashioned a rough wedding band from the soft metal. He took it to the riverbank and polished it in the sand.

Once he had it to his satisfaction, he sat Mary at the table and placed it on the third finger of her left hand. He said, "Now we are truly married, and everyone can see that we are. When we get back to civilization, it may be important. We will take care of the paperwork later.She was happy with the ring and let him know without delay in the way that women let their men know.

The song says, "May brings tiny buds and blossoms" and that is exactly what happened. Before long, Josh came in with a bunch of fresh baby carrots and had found that there were radishes to be eaten. He had baby potatoes and some baby onions. They ate the radishes and used the rest in a fresh pot of stew. They had fresh meat, fresh vegetables and fresh stew. It was good. In fact, they both felt that life was good, not just the food.

After they ate, the four of them went for a walk. Josh, Mary, the dog and Little Josh inside of his mother relished the sunshine and warm day. Mary told him, "I could live here with you forever. We could raise our children here and teach them both the ways of civilization and the ways of the wilderness."

He was tempted to agree, but he thought it over. "No, I don't think it would work out. I don't have the lumber to build fifteen new additions to that old cabin."

She looked and him and saw his slight grin, "Why fifteen?"

He told her, "A kitchen, living room, storeroom, our bedroom and one for each of the children. I figure that comes to at least fifteen, maybe eighteen."

She slapped at his arm but missed because she was giggling so much.

CHAPTER 13

One night they had a serious talk. It was about the necessity of ceasing intercourse for a time. There was a question about how they would satisfy her intense craving for sex. He promised that he would enjoy taking care of that little problem as often as she wished.

She smiled and said, "I have a feeling you are going to be dining at 'the Y' quite a lot."

"That is something I look forward to," he told her. "You know I have to shave your pubic hair when the baby is born. I think I should do it now and keep it shaved at least until after Little Josh is born." She giggled and agreed.

Using the big Bowie knife for such a delicate job was tricky. He honed it well on a strap of rawhide and began. Josh was very careful not to nick her tender skin. He was perspiring from the concentration and effort when he was through. He tested his handiwork with his tongue to make sure he got every little hair. She made him finish what he started when he tested.

Spring came with a rush. One day it was cold and blistery, and the very next it was warm. The weather held, and spring rains made the garden grow as never before. Having removed so many weeds and loosening the soil certainly helped. Josh saw to it that the garden was free of weeds at all times. It was a matter of pride.

June came and so did Mary's time for delivery. Her water broke while she was out helping Josh in the garden. Soon after that, she went into labor. They had practiced breathing exercises in preparation, but she still had to have a hard piece of jerky to bite down on toward the end. Little Josh was born by her watch at 12:21 pm.

There was a small surprise for them in the form of a little hand trying to grasp Little Josh's foot: out came another baby, a little girl. Josh was beside himself with joy and as busy as a bee building a hive trying to take care of both babies and the mother at the same time. Both babies started crying, which confused him more. He used some fish line to tie off the cords and cut them with his knife. He gave both a bath and dried them with a shirt.

Mary was smiling from ear to ear as she lay on the bed. The perspiration from her efforts beaded on her face and arms. Josh wiped her down with a cool cloth and put one infant on each side of her. They immediately began suckling, one on each breast.

Josh really wished he had a camera to take that picture. He thought it was the most beautiful sight he had ever seen. He was not ashamed of the tears of joy he felt running down his face.

He picked up a long stick he had been using as a "walking stick" and carved a notch in it. Each and every day he would carve a new notch in his "tally stick." That way he would be able to know exactly what day their twins were born so that when they reached someplace that had a calendar, all he had to do was count the days back to their birth.

One more chore was left to do. He was prepared to weigh the twins so someday that data could be recorded. During the winter he had built two slings and tied them to a stick. He would put a baby in one bag and stones in the other. There was a notch at the exact center of his weighing stick. He placed first Little Josh in a bag and balanced the weight with stones. It took 8 stones and some small pebbles to balance him. He marked the stones and pebbles and put them aside. He did the same with Little Mary. He reused the same stones but marked them differently. It took six stones and a few more pebbles to measure her weight. Measuring them was easier; he just measured them beside a stick and marked each one's length with his knife.

Soon after birth, the placenta was discharged. Josh was prepared and caught the material in a pan. He took it out and put it in the toilet hole. Early in the fall he had gathered pounds of cattails from a nearby marsh. They were hung high in the house. He got them down and instructed her how to use them as menstrual pads the way the Indian women did in the old days.

A cattail has a seed pod about six inches long and once

taken apart is soft and absorbent, quite similar to cotton in appearance, only much more fine.

Life settled into a busy routine. Preparations to leave when Mary was able to travel and taking care of the babies took most of their time. They had decided it would be best to leave as soon as the river went down to its normal size. That would be about the middle of July. They planned to travel slowly and take it easy. Josh made both Mary and himself front packs for the babies, each large enough for two. While taking on nourishment they would have to be with their mother. He planned to carry them on his chest much of the time.

They were almost ready to leave when tragedy struck in a big way. Josh was out hunting and scouting the river when a piece of the riverbank gave way under him. He fell some ten feet and landed on the rocks beside the stream. He was knocked unconscious for a few minutes. When he came to, he realized that his leg was broken below the knee. A rock that fell when the bank gave way had hit his leg.

He crawled to some driftwood nearby and found a sturdy stick to use as a crutch. He struggled to his feet and began slowly making his way back to the cabin. It was less than a hundred yards, but it seemed as though he had traveled for miles by the time he got there. During the entire time his jaws were clamped against the pain.

Mary had no idea what to do. She felt so helpless and lost. She began to panic. Josh saw the look and told her, "Don't worry; we will handle this one step at a time." He sat down on the ground and had her pull his foot as hard as she could pull. He heard and felt his bones settle back into place. He felt fortunate that it was a clean break.

As he instructed Mary, she gathered straight sticks and brought out soft deerskin. He had her first wrap his leg in deerskin and tie it on. Then she distributed the sticks on another piece of buckskin an inch apart. She tied them in position with the "pigging strings." She wrapped them around his leg and pulled them tight, tying the ends together. Lastly she wrapped another piece of hide over them, tying the makeshift splint tightly around his leg with wet pigging strings. As the wet leather dried, it would make the splint hold his leg in place. At last she helped him up and into the house.

Josh was on the bed with his leg slightly raised. Mary sat beside him. He said, "I will have to heal a little before we can leave. I would say a month at the most."

Mary told him, "It will take at least six weeks for that bone to mend in the best of circumstances. I had a broken arm once and was in the cast longer than two months."

Josh looked at her and saw that she was very tired from the exertion of fixing the cast and all that she did to help. He decided that traveling with the two infants would be too hard on her. She would endure and not complain, but it would exhaust her and make her susceptible to any kind of ailment.

He told her, "I think we should delay our trip until next spring when we have more time to get wherever we are going. We don't know how long it will take to get downriver to people and civilization."

Instead of looking disappointed, Mary looked relieved. She smiled, "You will have to get well soon anyway because we do need more room with four people and a dog in the house."

He surprised her by saying, "I already have something in mind, if you don't mind moving to a new neighborhood."

"Is it a bigger house, Mister McDougal?"

"You might say that. It is much bigger, but it is not actually a house."

After he told her his idea, Mary's eyes sparkled, "Why didn't we think of that last winter? We can move everything to the old mine. That's a wonderful idea."

Josh told her, "Everything can be moved. We have to think of a way to move the table and the bed, as well as the cook stove. I will have to take the bed apart and reassemble it. I think we can take the table as is. Other than that we can carry everything. It may take us a few days, but we can do it."

She looked at him thoughtfully. "You have already thought this through, haven't you? You already know how we are going to move. I will bet you even know how we can transport that cook stove. I know you think fast, but this took some planning."

He admitted as much. "I tend to plan ahead and consider possibilities. I considered it last winter and planned it all out as an alternative to where we were living. I almost suggested a move then."

Josh told Mary that he needed two forked sticks to make some crutches. She went out with the axe and cut down what he needed, two forked sticks about two inches in diameter at the fork. Josh whittled the lower part down to be about the same size, then smoothed the fork and padded it with leather. For comfort he sewed together two small bags and filled them with Mary's cattail fluff. He tied them onto the forks for cushions. Three days in bed was enough. Josh was up and out of bed.

Because healing quickly was of paramount importance, Josh tried not to strain his leg in any way; it would only delay healing. So many men think they are not tough if they sit back and let a broken bone heal. Many times they end up being much worse off than if they had taken care of their injury properly.

Mary unwrapped his leg about every other day, washed it and massaged it with bear grease to keep the makeshift cast from chafing. She soaked the outer wrapping and strings so they would tighten up again afterward. She made him stay on the bed until the wrapping was dry again. Josh did a lot of the babysitting and cooking while Mary took care of the garden and made a few preparations for their move. She also took over the hunting duties.

Mary brought home several deer over the next three weeks. Josh dried the meat and did what he could to tan the hides. He made her a buckskin shirt and a skirt that hung down below her knees. He made himself a buckskin shirt and pants outfit. In the end he had made two complete outfits for each of them. The clothes they brought from the airplane wreck had worn out, and the cloth was being used for other things.

He sewed together little outfits for the twins. Being babies it did not take much hide. He thought about it and made each of them three outfits, each set a little larger than the last. He reasoned that the children would grow into them.

Mary had been out with the bow for somewhat of a longer period of time one day. Hunting in close to the cabin was not fruitful anymore, so she was obliged to go further into the forest to get meat.

Josh began to worry and prepared to go look for her. He was just leaving on his mission when she appeared, bubbling over with excitement. She had not brought back any game so he assumed it was something else that made her so happy.

It didn't take long to find out what she had on her mind. "Josh, oh, Josh. I found it. I found our new home. We will not move to the mine at all. We will move to a much better place."

Josh poured her some cool peppermint tea they had brewed from peppermint leaves that grew near the river. He told her, "Calm down a little before you burst. When you are relaxed, I want to know all about it."

She sat in a chair with Josh in the other chair and began her tale. There was still excitement and a bit of wonder in her voice.

CHAPTER 14

She began: "I was hunting a little further from camp than usual and was about to turn back when I saw a small trickle of water. I was thirsty so I knelt to get a drink and discovered that the water was slightly warm. Out of curiosity I follow it up a slight grade and came to the opening of a cave. It was almost hidden in the trees, but the opening was big enough for me to enter comfortably beside the little stream.

Inside the cave there was a pool of water near one wall. It is a big cave, and the floor is flat as a pancake for the most part. I explored and found that it has three good-sized rooms, each bigger than this cabin. The pool is about four feet wide and a good eight feet long. I think it is at least two feet deep, and the water is warm. I cannot think of anything better for our home. It is about the same distance from here as the old mine is, only in the opposite direction."

Josh thought for a moment and said, "Well, then I guess we move to the Ritz Hotel of the Wilderness. You didn't fall and hit your head or anything? This is all real?"

She assured him that it was real with a kiss and told him, "Husband, you are teasing me again." The kids were looking for a meal so she sat down to nurse them.

Josh rigged up a harness for himself and one for the dog. He built two travois, one for himself and a small one for the dog. He reasoned that the husky in his ancestry would make him easy to train. It did. The dog took to the harness and the job as though he was born for it.

At the end of the month they began to move. With Mary carrying the children and Josh with the stove on his travois, they started out. Josh used his crutches and his good leg to pull the heavy load. The dog had a load of jerky in a deer hide bag and their bedding. They rested frequently and took over an hour to make it just short of a mile to the new quarters.

For the first time Josh saw what Mary had described and

noted that it was a very accurate description. He did note that the entrance was mostly blocked off by a landslide at one time, and there were several places where he could see daylight along the front wall. He would have to patch most of those holes in some way, but one would be the outlet for the rusty old stovepipe that went with the stove. He told her, "Sweetheart, this is even better than your description. We will have to kill a couple more bears and make bear rugs for our mansion."

On that first day of moving, they made eight trips in a twelve-hour day. The first was the stove, then the bed, with the table following. Josh wanted to move all the heavy stuff first while he had more strength. The rest of the trips were much easier for them and went more quickly. There was little to be moved the following day. When harvest time came, Josh would use his and the dog's travois again to move all of the vegetables and produce. In the meantime, he thought his would be handy for transporting the game he shot instead of often having to make two trips for the bigger kills.

Josh carried Mary over the threshold again while she held the babies. He bade them welcome to their new home and kissed each of them.

The first night they made do with jerky because they were so tired, and it was so late. The stove was not set up, and they did not want to build a fire on their floor or just outside. They went to sleep curled up in each other's arms.

The next morning Josh set up the stove and chimney. He made sure it was level and started a fire for breakfast. While Mary cooked, he took the bed to the room she designated as the bedroom and set it up. He worked in the dim light from the entrance and the lamp she was using in the other room. He thought about what they could do for light in their new home. The only fuel for the lamp that remained was what was in the lamp, and it was full. Conservatively he thought it would last a month. Josh and the dog went back for the final load while Mary busied herself arranging her new home to her liking.

They designated one room for storage, one for a bedroom and the big room as their living room. The babies got a warm bath in the pool that suddenly became their bathtub, and so did the adults. It was pure luxury to them.

They took turns hunting and babysitting. Their larder expanded to include deer, elk, and bear meat. They avoided the larger bears as much as possible since their meat would be tougher, and they were much more dangerous. They chose younger elk and deer. Much of their meat was rabbit because Josh wanted their fur. He made linings for their shoes and coats for winter. There was so much game that they could be choosy.

He chose a place near the entrance to their cave, built a big rack for drying meat, and constructed a large table to be used in cutting up the meat. He made a wide circle of stones below the rack for his smoke fire.

Josh's leg healed rapidly, and he soon forgot his crutches. They sat in a corner never to be used again.

He did most of the hunting from then on.

The harvest from berry bushes was abundant because this year they were picking them as they ripened. They had a large variety of fruit including some wild plums, chokecherries, blueberries, huckleberries, salmon berries, blackberries, and raspberries. They dried all of them for later use.

The yield from the garden was abundant. The potatoes were larger and more plentiful. The beans turned out to be three different varieties and yielded three full bags that easily held two bushels each. Carrots, beets and onions were in abundance. Their storage room became full. Josh was careful not to harvest every last plant. He left some to go to seed.

In the period of time that the old miner had lived, there were no hybrid plants. Hybrids cannot reproduce themselves. These vegetables could. Josh cultivated the garden, and once the seeds were ripe, he planted them and let nature raise him a new garden in the spring.

Josh was able to make a crib with a soft bear hide for a cushion for the babies and a playpen with a bear fur on which to play. He built a wooden barrier around the bathtub so the kids would not fall into it when they began to crawl. Overall they were ready for winter when it hit.

The first snow of the year came about the first of September. It was only about four inches and melted quickly. Indian summer set in with warm, balmy days and cold nights. It was the time of year for relaxation and enjoyment of nature.

Josh wanted more rugs in their "house" and went out looking for bear. He found a big brown bear that did not take kindly to the arrow poking into his heart. Josh was obliged to climb up on some rocks to avoid the enraged, dying bear. It took several minutes and two more arrows for the animal's heart to finally stop. Josh went to get his travois. He gutted his kill but left the hide alone until he got his kill home. He strung it up and skinned it, then quartered it and took the meat to the table he had made near the drying rack where they made jerky. Josh busied himself setting strips of bear on the rack for jerky.

Mary did the job of scraping the excess away from the hide and laid it out flat to dry. The "rug" would be stiff when it dried and covered a large area of the floor. They needed one more rug.

They got that last one at the place where Josh had dressed out the bear. A cougar was sniffing around the leavings when Josh approached downwind. He had a habit of making little or no noise when he hunted, and the cat was not aware of his presence.

The dog approached the cat and challenged it for the entrails. The cougar was concentrating on the potential fight with the dog when an arrow penetrated his heart. It was a big cat and made a wonderful rug for the parents' bedroom.

Josh cooked some of the meat and served it to Mary. When she asked, he told her it tasted like chicken, with a grin on his face. In actual fact it was very good but tasted nothing like chicken. He told her, "You have eaten beaver tail, and that was a delicacy of the trippers long ago. Now you will eat the other meat that they felt was just as good and some thought even better tasting."

There was one thing more to do before winter. Josh wanted to have some fish. He went down to the river, which was very low at that time of the year. He grappled and caught large rainbow trout. Each one he cleaned and used his knife to filet. He had to marvel that the Bowie was still sharp after all he had used it for and how harshly it had been abused. By the time he felt he had enough fish, he had a backpack full. He carried nearly a hundred pounds of fish to his smoking rack. They would have smoked fish for the winter.

He dug the hole and reconstructed the outhouse fairly close to the cave and under the trees, but he was careful to put it downwind. He had gone back to the cabin and took down the outhouse, filled the hole, and transported the pieces to the new location on his travois. The trees sheltered it from the snow to some extent and made it easier for them to make the daily – at least – trip.

Their children began to learn to crawl and thoroughly enjoyed the big bear rug. They learned quickly that moving off that rug would hurt their knees, and it was colder than on the rug so they never left it. It was a built-in babysitter. Their progress as infants seemed to the couple to be rapid and developing at an early age. Fortunately, neither child had become sick in any way.

Mary sent Josh out to gather cattails many times. That is what she used for diapers inside a pair of panties she made for each of them. Josh had brought back every cattail he could find in two marshes. They felt that they had their winter's supply.

Josh put a long pole about three inches in diameter across the top of the entrance and hung a hide over it making the hide secure to the pole. It was long enough to reach the ground and allowed them to put rocks at the bottom so the wind would not blow open their door. He stuffed the excess holes in the front wall with a mixture of mud and grass.

They enjoyed two more weeks of good weather and often strolled in the woods enjoying themselves. They took picnic lunches and made real outings of their walks. While their babies slept under the trees all content and full of food, the couple made love.

The darkness of the cave was a problem because they ran out of kerosene. The lamp was useless until Josh took off the top and the wick mechanism. He filled the lamp base with melted bear grease and used the wick for a candlewick. It gave them light but not very much of it. He had to think of something else.

When they took the lids off the stove, the exposed fire made a lot of light, and the smoke still gravitated toward the smoke pipe because of the good draft. It would have to do until he could think of something else. Lighting torches was out because the smoke would fill the cave and choke them. Josh decided to try it anyway.

He knocked away the chinking he had put in two very high holes in the front wall and lit a pitch-filled stick about four feet long. A good bright flame lit up the inside of the cave very well. The smoke traveled along the ceiling and out those two vent holes. He jammed the unlit end of his torch into a crack in the wall near his vents and let it burn. They had light. Before snow fell, he went out and gathered a good many torches with pine pitch imbedded in them. He usually burned two torches at a time for a lot more light in their home.

Both the storeroom and the bedroom were dimly lit by the torches. This satisfied the couple. If they needed light in another room, they simply carried a torch. For some reason the smoke always gravitated along the ceiling and out those vent holes. It was pitch dark inside during the night, but the babies were sleeping all night and not disturbed by it being so very dark. Josh and Mary began to learn Braille on each other's body. That was the fun part.

The first storm came casually in the night. In the morning there was at least a foot of snow on the ground. Under the trees there was less, so walking out was easy.

Mary was more than happy with the rabbit fur coat she wore. It reached almost to the ground. The fur in her boots kept her feet warm. The cave was warm because of the cook stove, torches, and the warm water "tub."

Josh heard bear, both singular and plural, come sniffing around the cave looking for a place to hibernate. When they smelled human scent, they left. Josh guessed that word must have gone out to avoid him. They had five bear rugs on the floor, two bear blankets on their bed, one in the playpen, and another under the kids in the crib. The kid's blanket was made of rabbit hides sewn together. As always, Mary sewed while Josh poked holes in the hide with the point of the Bowie knife.

Once more they settled in for a long winter. They needed nothing because everything was right there in their home. The only reason to go out into the cold was to go to the bathroom. They did not feel right about going bottomless around the children so they usually wore something. The pants and skirt Josh fashioned from buckskin. They were usually topless unless going out.

One day Josh decided he had not taken a through enough look at their cave. He took one of the torches and walked around the walls and into all the rooms. When he got to the storeroom, which was much larger than the bedroom, he discovered a hole in the wall. It was more like a wide crack and large enough to enter.

Inside it was like a long corridor, long and narrow. It seemed he walked for a long way twisting and turning along the path. He could feel air on his face, and his torch indicated a flow or air. Eventually he saw light ahead. He went and looked out into a different valley and a different forest. The opening was small, and so he did not try to force his way outside. He did stick his head out of the hole and looked around. The opening was on the side of a sheer cliff. He knew now why there was such a good draft in the cave that caused the smoke to so readily go out of the vent holes.

He made his way back to his family and told what he had discovered. It was interesting but in no way affected them. It only answered a question Josh had been thinking about concerning smoke.

One day the dog suddenly stood and looked at the door. He was growling, and the hair stood up all along his back. A cougar poked its head in beside the door and looked them over. It stood for several seconds before leaving. Josh guessed he had satisfied his curiosity.

That was the only incident of note for the entire winter. They enjoyed comfort and peace throughout. There was a nice spell in February again, followed by several more weeks of severe weather. Gale force winds twice blew down their door, and snow was falling into the entrance. By the middle of April, things had quieted down, but the snow did not leave until mid-May. The weather still threatened, and snow flurries came frequently. June brought the real spring with it.

It was a good thing the weather broke. They were almost out of wood for the fire, torches, and food. They were becoming concerned.

CHAPTER 15

One night they put the kids to bed and decided to stay up a little later. They began to talk about the journey ahead and about how far they had to go. Josh took Mary out and read her the stars. He could not tell exactly what their longitude and latitude was, but he could tell they were a lot further north than he had figured at first. He calculated it out in his head and told her. "I believe we have from two to three hundred miles before we get to anywhere that we can call civilization."

Mary told him, "It would be very hard on the children. They are just now turning a year old and are still toddlers. We would have to carry those two most of the way, and then there is the problem of potty training. I think we should stay right here until they can travel and take care of their personal needs themselves. Even at two they will need to be carried a lot."

Josh was surprised at her suggestion. "Do you mean you would not mind staying for another year?"

She hugged him and said, "I would not mind if we stayed forever. I have never been happier in my life. I feel so free and yet so loved. I know we will have to leave here someday, but do we have to rush it?"

They decided to stay until their children were better able to handle the rigors of the trail.

Josh began to prepare their home for the next winter while taking care of present needs. He stopped by and worked in the garden whenever he was out hunting. The cleared area had become a prime place to get deer since spring had arrived.

Their situation improved as Josh added more rugs, built up their larder and supplied more meat for the table. He had to build a larger bed for the twins since they were growing out of their crib. Little Josh started out a little bigger than his sister did, and that is the way it remained. Little Mary began to resemble her mother more each day, and Little Josh looked and acted just like his daddy.

Hardships were few and far between as they lived out the

summer, enjoying every second of their lives together. They went on numerous picnics and excursions. Josh spent most of his time fishing, hunting, or tending the garden. The twins grew in strength and soon were walking and talking. Little Mary, it seemed, would never shut up; Little Josh seldom had anything to say, but when he did, it meant something.

The two children seemed to be "one with the animals," so to speak. It was not unusual to see them feeding a squirrel or letting birds sit on their hands while they had a chirping contest. They petted fawns and even baby bears. None of the parent animals seemed to mind. It was as though they knew they were all just babies and would do no harm.

One day Josh saw a rather small animal approach Little Mary. It made a hissing noise, and the little girl backed away. The animal had a white stripe down each side of its nose up to his eyes. It was very much all fur except for the head. Little Josh ran over to his dad and said, "Mary has mean animal."

Josh took one look and grabbed his bow. Before anyone realized what was happening, there were four arrows in the animal. Mary came out and wanted to know what happened. Little Mary was crying so she picked her up and comforted her.

Josh said, "Remember when I told you that there are exceptions to the rule that animals only kill for food? Well, that animal is a wolverine, and it is the exception. It is born with a chip on its shoulder and kills just to be killing. They are vicious mean animals and are to be avoided as much as possible."

Knowing that they would be leaving in a year, more than likely, Josh revamped his travois to make it much narrower; it would go along the trail much better. He built two seats, one for each kid, on the travois with leather. He gave them rides on it and carried them through the forest, down game trails, and all the way to the garden. They soon learned that they had to remain still when in their seats. It was an easy pull for Josh and a lot of fun for the kids.

One day Little Josh put the dog's harness on the dog and hooked up his travois. He laid on the travois as the dog pulled him around through the forest. He put his sister on, and the dog pulled her. He never ran, just walked them around. He seemed to like doing it. Eventually the kids found a way to have him cart both of them at the same time.

Work came in the form of making a lot of jerky and other preparations for winter. Josh brought meat in frequently that he turned into jerky. They ate fresh meat, but most of it was smoked and jerked before it could spoil. About twice a week Josh took the dog to the garden and had him haul a bunch of produce home.

He found and stockpiled a great number of the sticks he used for torches. There were enough so they could burn two a day for a long time without having to replenish their supply. He chopped and stockpiled wood both inside and outside of the cave. They spent endless hours preparing and drying vegetables and berries they had picked in the fall.

No pioneer had ever been more prepared for winter storms.

There were stacks and stacks of buckskin bags filled to capacity in the storeroom. They organized the room into departments according to the product the bags contained.

They made new clothes for the kids twice during the summer and stockpiled sheets of buckskin for making more during the winter. They seemed to grow out of clothes faster than new ones could be made. Josh made moccasins with rabbit fir linings for winter for all of them. He made new linings for his boots and Mary's. The kids got rabbit fur coats. Josh's winter coat was made from a bear hide.

When winter came, they were ready. They would miss being able to traipse through the woods, but they would be well fed and sheltered. For entertainment Josh and Mary told the children stories. Mostly they told them the nursery rhymes and stories from their own childhood. Mary sang children's songs and Irish ballads. Now and then Josh would join by whistling in tune with the song.

For Christmas Mary made Little Mary a doll out of buckskin and stuffed it with old rags of what were once clothes. Josh made carvings of animals for Little Josh and used berry juice to stain them the right colors. He carved a head for the doll

Mary made, as well as hands and feet. Once Little Mary's doll was finished, it looked almost like a real baby.

They taught the Christmas story to their children and told of the way people decorated trees for their homes. When asked why they didn't have a decorated tree, Josh had them get into their warm clothes and showed them the frost on the limbs of many trees and how they sparkled when the sunlight hit them. He told them, "The Great Spirit decorated lots of them just for you."

It was a joyous Christmas with a feast of roast venison that Josh went out into the deep snow and killed. It was a very cold day, and before he got home from that outing, he felt the beginnings of frostbite. If his calculations were correct, they were still a lot closer to the Arctic Circle than he wanted.

It grew so cold that they could hear the branches of trees snap as the ice inside of them expanded. Some were so loud that it sounded like gunshots. That night they were visited by a pair of lynx. They woke up in the morning to find them sleeping near the pond inside the cave. Josh saw where they had pushed the door hide aside and entered. Once he lit a torch and stirred the fire in the stove, they woke up. Josh kept an eye on them, but never bothered them. They ignored the human animal.

Once his fire was established, he went into the storeroom and took a big handful of jerky. He tossed it to the cats and watched as they ate breakfast. He began talking to them in a low voice so as not to excite them.

Little Josh woke and crawled out of bed. He started to go over to the two lynx when Josh told him to stop. "Those are wild animals, and they can be very dangerous. You need to leave them alone."

Little Josh said, "No, daddy, they are my friends. This is Fuzzy and that is Muzzy. We played together last summer when they were kittens." He demonstrated by holding out his hand and calling them. They got up and started rubbing against the child, just as a house cat would when it wanted affection.

Mary came out of the bedroom just as her daughter came over and started hugging one of the cats. She was shocked and worried until Josh told her, "Evidently those two lynx are pets of our kids. Little Josh told me they were playing with each other last summer when the cats were kittens. I think we have house guests."

The dog, which was very protective when it came to the children, did not seem to mind the presence of the two lynx at all. He accepted their presence as normal. In fact he played with both animals. For the next few days they furnished a lot of entertainment for the family.

The cold snap finally broke, and Fuzzy and Muzzy left as suddenly as they had appeared. Josh wondered what other visitors they would have coming to visit and getting a free meal or two. He did not have long to wait.

They heard a commotion just outside the door. When Josh investigated, he saw an eagle having a fight with a wolf. Because the eagle had a damaged wing, the wolf was winning. Josh settled the argument, and the wolf made another rug. They brought the wounded bald eagle into the cave.

Little Mary talked to it and caressed it as Josh and Mary made a splint for the broken wing and washed the bird's wounds with a solution of herbs Josh made. Of course, the eagle could not fly, and it seemed to like the attention from both children. Josh made a place for their new houseguest. The kids fed it dried vegetables and small pieces of jerky.

The children named the eagle "Eddy" and started teaching it to respond to the name. It never left the bed Josh had made for it for a week. Eventually it began to walk around and even hop up on things. One morning when Josh got up to start their routine, he noticed that the eagle was missing from its usual place. On looking around he found it sleeping on the foot of the bed with the twins.

Eddy learned his name and followed the kids around like a puppy. When the kids would go separate ways, the eagle would stand and look from one to the other before he chose which to follow. There seemed to be no preference, and the children had a lot of fun guessing which he would choose.

Walking Out of the Canadian Wilderness

Eventually they removed the splint, and the eagle tried out his wing. When he spread those wings, he was at least six feet long from wing tip to wing tip. He began to try out his wings by flying from one side of the room to the next. He did not seem anxious to leave his comfortable surroundings. He stayed with them until May when the weather turned a little warmer.

One day they heard an eagle's cry outside of the cave. Suddenly Eddy became excited, so Josh had him perch on his arm and took him outside. The eagle immediately flew off and joined a female eagle that was calling to him. Josh told the children and Mary, "That was his wife. Eagles mate for life, and she must have spent a lot of time looking for her mate."

June and spring finally arrived. Chinook winds took away most of the snow, and the family had a conference.

They all agreed that their home was wonderful, but that it would be nice to find a place further south where the winters were not so harsh. They decided to move. It was less an attempt to leave the wilderness than it was an attempt to move to an area more suitable for human habitation.

CHAPTER 16

The family packed up what they needed for the trip and were ready to leave at any time. The children were ready for the trail and become more and more excited about the trip all the time. They were about to have their second birthday. Josh decided to say good-bye to the cave and start their new adventure when he counted 728 days on his tally stick. It was exactly 2 years since the twins were born.

Josh had a lot to carry on his travois. It was bulky and heavy. He carried the bedrolls as well as food, clothes, some of the kitchenware and his "hidden keepsakes." The dog pulled a travois the contained only a fur. He would be carrying the kids when they got tired of walking. Mary had a light pack that consisted mostly of plastic bags filled with cattail fluff, more food and the kid's rabbit fur bedding. Josh brought along the axe and shovel as well. They would be handy on the trail.

Their first day on the trail was to see how much endurance they had; it was somewhat of a shakedown time. Toward the end of the day, the kids were riding on the dog's travois. Their excitement had settled down, having walked quite a bit, and they were tired. They slept in the furs on the travois. They made about ten miles before they camped.

Josh was not displeased. He praised Mary for her endurance and determination. Mary played with the kids while Josh went into the woods and came back with three grouse. He set up the fire and roasted the birds for their evening meal. By dark they were in bed like an old married couple. She was on one side, he on the other and the kids in the middle. Everyone was warm although it was a cold night.

In the morning Josh got up first and built a fire. He went out, killed a couple of rabbits for their breakfast, and was cooking them when his family finally arose and got themselves ready for the day. The sun was still low in the sky when they were back on the trail. Josh used his tally stick as a walking stick. He cut one for Mary, and she was surprised how much easier it was to walk with it, although she did not really seem to be using the stick much at all. When they walked, both children had their own little sticks and mimicked their parents.

About noon they stopped and ate some jerky while they rested. Josh heard a faint rumble in the distance, but thought it was a storm way off somewhere. He kept an eye out just in case. The sky turned grey, and Josh started seeking some place to camp while it rained.

He saw a thick growth of fir trees and sought the shelter he knew they could provide. He used the axe and cut one small tree after another. He tied a pole between two trees about 6 feet from the ground to make a cross member and leaned poles against it. This he covered with branches. They got under the lean-to just in time for the downpour. When the rain did not stop and it started to become dusk, he went out and cut more small trees. He built another lean-to facing the first and covered it thickly with branches. He used the same cross member to make the second lean-to so he had only to put branches down the ridge to keep the rain from coming in there. When he crawled inside, he saw that they had just enough room to spread out their bedroll and store their packs. He quickly got out of his wet clothes and dried himself off with an old shirt.

They ate jerky for dinner and went to bed. Once more the children had the middle with the adults on the edges. Josh breathed a sigh of contentment and relief that his shelter did not leak. He thought, "Let it rain; we are safe and dry."

Josh woke up to a strange noise just after daybreak the next morning. The dog was sleeping at the foot of the bed and two raccoons were standing there, or rather sitting, looking in. They seemed to be talking to each other. The chatter finally woke the dog, and the raccoons scurried off when he let out a low growl. The dog and Josh went back to sleep. It was still raining.

An hour later another low growl woke Josh. He looked and saw a wolf just about to jump a fawn that was lying down. Josh put an arrow right in front of the wolf's nose. It stuck in a tree and quivered. That startled the wolf and scared him away.

He noticed that the rain had stopped, and the sun was

79

shining. They moistened some dried berries and had some more jerky for breakfast. They were on their way shortly after Josh dismantled the shelter and scattered the many branches about so there was little evidence of their having been there.

Josh seriously considered building a raft and floating down the river, but he was sure there would be some dangerous rapids ahead and did not want to risk the lives of his wife and children. They continued to follow the right side of the river, now fifty feet wide. He saw that the valley they were going down turned toward the west a little and thought about cutting across to save some distance. He decided to stay with the river.

A mile later just as the valley turned, the river suddenly disappeared. All of the water simply vanished into the ground. There was not a sign of even a trickle of water anywhere. They had no choice but to continue down the valley.

Something bothered Josh about that river. He remembered reading about one that did the very same thing and reappeared some miles away in the form of a giant spring. He hoped it was not the same river since his memory told him the "Disappearing River" was far up in the Canadian Northwest Territory. It would be at least two hundred miles from there to the nearest settlement.

As the valley descended, the terrain become more difficult to travel. They found themselves having to climb down steep rocky places that were so steep they had to get on their hands and knees and back down slowly for fifty feet or more. They traversed around some places that would be impossible for them to climb. They traveled many miles but only gained five in a straight line. They reached the bottom of the valley just before nightfall overtook them. There was a small stream and an overhang that afforded them a little shelter. The stream yielded some good fish for their evening meal.

The next morning they were getting ready to move on when Mary asked, "Do you think we could find a good place and rest up for a day or two? I think the little ones could use it, and I know I could."

Josh told her, "Today we will look for a place."

Knowing that they would take a holiday and rest seemed to perk everyone up a bit. They made good time across a broad flat area. They came across a meadow that had been nearly grazed clean by a vast herd of elk. Josh saw the signs they had left behind and told Mary.

On the edge of that meadow was an old Indian camp. They found several arrowheads that would be valuable to Josh for his arrows. They could see the circles of stones where the village fires had burned at one time. As they moved on, Josh made a mental note to find out what tribe had occupied this area.

Later in the day Josh saw an ideal location for a rest camp. He said nothing, just stopped suddenly. He turned away from the stream and walked a few yards. There was a level spot that was almost completely bare of trees. It was a small glen about twenty yards across and probably thirty long. The ground seemed soft, yet dry, and there was plenty of material to build a good-sized double lean-to similar to the one he had built in haste a couple days earlier.

He set to work cutting and trimming the uprights with a fork at one end to hold the cross member he cut. This time the uprights would be strong because he planted six of them at intervals as though they were posts. The two middle ones were high with the outer ones about a foot and a half lower. The cross members were larger to carry a heavier load. He cut and placed poles leaning over the high cross member and laying on the lower ones. He had poles nearly side by side on both sides of the lean-to. He put all the branches from the poles on the lean-to and was very satisfied. This one was much larger than the other and easily held everything with room to spare. The construction took the form of a canopy more than a lean-to. It had taken them the rest of the day. They had jerky for dinner.

The next morning Josh shot a deer. They needed fresh meat. He found some wild onions and brought them in although he had dried onions in his pack. He produced a pot and filled it with water. Mary mixed dried vegetables, dried potatoes with cut up pieces of venison and onion, and made a delicious stew.

While Mary was preparing dinner and the kids were playing

with the dog, Josh busied himself putting arrowheads on his arrows. He was anxious to try them.

Josh laid out the hide, scraped off the hair, and cut it into long continuous strips about three-eighths of an inch wide. In the next few days he used them to make a rope. He used a four-strand braid and pulled each layer of braid tight, stretching the green hide as much as he possibly could. The project would take a lot of his time while they rested up. In the end he would have a leather rope. It was not as long as he would have liked, but it would come in handy. Several times he had wished he had a rope during the last couple of days.

Being only two years old, the children were on solid foods, but still could not chew meat as well as the adults. They chose to eat the soft pieces of vegetables and broth. They wanted more and more. The twins were very hungry. They slept soundly in their own bedroll while Josh and Mary made love for the first time since they had started on the trail. It was a great relief of tension for the two of them.

During the night, there was a great racket outside their shelter. Josh could tell the dog was having a quarrel with something, but it was too dark to tell what. Of course, the family was awake from the noise. He told Mary to stay there, and he would take care of it. He yelled and went toward the noise, a foolish move in anyone's book. It could have gotten him killed by whatever was fighting the dog. His yelling as he approached worked. Whatever was fighting the dog took off. The next morning Josh inspected the dog. He seemed to be unaffected by his confrontation, but there was some blood on his muzzle. It was not his.

Josh tracked down the wounded coyote and put it out of its misery. He had just finished skinning the animal when he heard his wife scream. He ran into camp and almost ran smack into a big cougar. The dog was fending it off as best he could without being hit by one of those deadly paws. But the cat had his eye on Mary.

It was crouched and ready to spring when Josh's arrow entered its side just behind the front leg. The arrow went through the heart and out the other side of the animal. Josh thought he must have really pulled the strings back that time. The strings were no longer made of fish line; they were now one string, and it was sinew from a deer.

The mountains are full of dangers, and one must be on guard at all times. A rock can roll out from under your foot. A tree or a large limb may fall from way up in a tree. You could meet an animal with rabies, and a mad animal will attack anything. You could slip and fall or a section of a bank could give way as it did with Josh. Cougars will not usually attack a human, but it does happen. Josh opened the cat's mouth and found that the old animal has lost most of its teeth. It was only trying to survive by attacking the easiest prey. One leg was deformed by arthritis, and the coat was not in good shape. Josh felt he did the cat a favor. It was dying from old age and would have died a horrible death at the hands, or rather claws, of another predator.

The twins were behind their mother so the dog went to them. They were wrestling with the dog. The dog seemed to enjoy the two little ones climbing all over him. Josh let the dog do the babysitting while he held Mary and reassured her. Before long, he felt that she was enjoying the reassuring a lot more than being upset or frightened.

Josh pulled the dead cat into the woods. Some wolf or coyote would enjoy the meal. The hide of the coyote and that of the cougar became a part of Josh's now much longer leather rope.

It began raining and rained for two days. The family had plenty to eat and spent their time inside the shelter. It was a time of naps and playing with the children. Josh and Mary were able to make love while the twins napped on several occasions. By the time it stopped raining and the sun came out, they were anxious to be back on the trail.

The little stream had become a real "gully washer." If they had made their camp close to the stream, they would have been washed out. As it was, the stream's width and current forced them to take a number of detours through thick brush. To make it easier for his wife and children, Josh went ahead and used the big Bowie as a machete to cut a trail through the thick brush.

They came out of the valley only to see more mountains ahead. The middle of the valley consisted of a big lake with the stream emptying into it. They were going to be obligated to walk around the lake to try to find the outlet. Josh explained that it was the only way to find civilization or a place to build their new home. As long as they went in a southerly direction and followed water down, they would find the ideal place and maybe meet other people. He told Mary that they may be in for a very long hike. They camped by the lake, and everyone took a cold bath. Again they camped on a high spot, just in case the lake water got any higher. It did.

The following morning they found themselves on an island. During the night the lake expanded to include the area around the knoll. They decided to wait a day or two before attempting to go further. They watched as the water receded by the hour. By nightfall they moved their camp to higher ground further from the lake. In the morning they breakfasted on leftover stew and proceeded on their way.

The water in the middle of the lake seemed to be boiling. A very strong current from under the water made the lake bubble up. Mary asked what caused it. Josh told her, "I think we have found that river again. I think it comes up from the ground right here, and that is the reason for the lake. The outlet stream will be a river." Josh was relieved to see that he was right when they found the outlet for the lake.

Josh called Mary's attention to some large fish. "See how red those fish are? Those are salmon, and they come from the ocean and up the streams to spawn. As they continue upstream in fresh water, they slowly turn red like that. After they spawn, they will die." As they watched, they saw one dig a little depression with its nose and then deposit eggs in the hollow. Another fish came and sprayed a milky substance over the eggs.

Josh told her, "We have found their spawning grounds. What you just witnessed was a female and male laying and fertilizing their eggs. This has great meaning for us. This river is connected to the ocean, and civilization is definitely downstream there somewhere. It also means that we are at the end of the journey for those salmon and therefore more than likely a long way from any settlements."

CHAPTER 17

Mary took the news in stride. "Does that mean we will get to be on our little outing for a bit longer?" From Mary's statement, he knew what she really wanted was to find some form of civilization rather than stay in the mountains.

He told her, "At the rate we are traveling, I would guess we are averaging close to fifteen miles a day, not counting rest periods. It looks to me as though we can expect to be moving along for another two weeks to a month. We should be out of the mountains before winter sets in again. It is probably July. There should be two months of good weather yet."

The next three days were uneventful. They followed the river down and camped each night on high ground. It was in the afternoon of the third day that they discovered another pool of warm water. Mary informed Josh that they would camp right there even though it was early. The whole family spent an hour in the warm water. The twins began their first swimming lessons in that pool, and all four people were very happy. They camped there for three days. By the time they were ready to move on, both children could swim.

They regretted leaving that place. Mary observed that if they had to spend another winter in the wilderness, she hoped it would be next to such a place. Josh told her, "Next winter you will spend in my house."

"Oh", Mary said. "You own a house?"

Josh told her, "Just a little place outside of Missoula, Montana." What he did not tell her was that his "little place" once was a guest ranch, and the main building had six bedrooms, all with their own full bathroom and that the main room could accommodate over a hundred people comfortably. The kitchen and dining rooms were big enough to accommodate a large number of guests. It was huge and the grounds he had under title included several large three-bedroom cabins as well.

He had inherited it when he was just twenty-one. Renting

out those houses paid his taxes and utilities plus a little extra. A rental agency handled all of the details for him.

Josh went ahead as their trail narrowed, and so the subject was dropped. The river went over a falls of some fifty feet, and the little family had to make their way down a steep incline. They slipped and slid about thirty feet down a shale side hill to the floor of the valley below. The kids thought that was fun. He tied his rope to a tree at the top and eased everyone down slowly. He slid down rapidly with the coiled rope in his hands.

Downstream from the falls, they made camp. During the night they were all awakened by a noise that sounded for the entire world like a woman screaming. Mary was concerned until he told her it was a cougar looking for his mate. As the animal passed their camp, they could smell onions, the smell of a cougar. It was a smell familiar to all of them. Josh knew the animal was on the prowl and was glad he had not bothered them. The next day they spotted two cougars sunning themselves on a large rock. Josh commented, "It looks as though our cougar found what he wanted last night."

Mary laughed and used a free arm to hug Josh, "Me too. I wish them happiness and a long life together."

The fact that the cats were undisturbed by the presence of people, and the way every animal more or less just wandered out of their way told Josh that they were not used to people. They had never been hunted, and so therefore the family still had a long ways to go.

They came to a large meadow. It was covered by a large herd of elk. They detoured around so as not to disturb them, but it was to no avail. Something far to the other side spooked the herd. The entire herd was stampeding toward them.

Josh led his family uphill and found a place of refuge behind some big boulders. They watched as the herd stopped at the edge of the forest and bunched together. Young bulls surrounded the cows and calves, watching in all directions. Several big bulls with one in the forefront lined up on the far side and closely watched a pack of about ten wolves pass through the meadow. A few minutes later they were back to

87

grazing.

When evening arrived, Josh said they had made good time in spite of the delay. When he came back from catching some fish for dinner, he saw both kids and a calf elk together. They were petting the animal and talking to it. The old cow did not like it much, but kept her distance. Josh chuckled and wondered what they were telling that calf. Mary was watching to make sure no harm came to the kids, but she could hardly contain her chuckles. When the twins tired of the animal and walked away, the calf followed them. The cow made a noise, so the calf turned and went back to its mother.

Josh asked, "Where is the dog?"

Mary told him, "I thought he was with you."

Josh whistled and the dog appeared from the direction of the river. He was carrying a rabbit in his mouth. He laid it at Josh's feet and wagged his tail. Josh petted him and told him he was a smart and good dog. He seemed proud of himself.

Josh thought they would have to come up with a name for the animal eventually. He thought of how he had been a guardian for them and what a lifesaver he was. He named the dog Candy. Mary accepted the name, thinking Josh had a weird sense of humor.

There came a time that they were in a thunder and lightning storm. No rain but lots of lightning. Some people say that you should stay out of the forest during such a storm, but it is far from true. Lightning strikes the high objects as it seeks a ground. A person out on a prairie would be a high object in relation to his surroundings. Trees are struck because they are high objects. They waited for the rain that never came. Josh hoped that none of the lightning started a fire. His hopes were in vain. It was only half an hour later when they saw a great many animals running toward the northwest.

Cougars and deer ran together in their rush to safety from the fire that lightning had started. Other meat-eating predators ran beside the foliage-eating animals that were their natural prey. Even birds were flying away from the fire that burned and filled the air with smoke.

Josh led his family to follow the animals. He trusted the animals to lead them to safety. They congregated on a high hill that was barren of vegetation. The family joined the animals with the smell of smoke irritating their nostrils. They looked back and saw a fire burning under the trees and clearing out the dead timber and underbrush.

Some forest fires are "crown," meaning the fire is in the top of the trees and spreads very rapidly from treetop to treetop. Some are ground fires that burn out the underbrush and quickly die before they affect the big trees. They progress more slowly; this was one of those fires. They watched the fire's progress as it passed them. When the animals started leaving the hill, Josh led his family away, and they continued their journey.

They detoured around places that were still burning and others that were still hot so their progress was slow, but eventually they came out of the burned area. The whole family was covered with soot and ash. They hoped they would find a place to clean up.

Later in the evening it started raining. Josh found shelter under a very large rock that was on top of two smaller ones and therefore had a sort of cave under it. They waited and knew the forest fire would be extinguished. Josh went out into the rain and let it rinse him and his clothes for a while. He stripped and let the rain wash him. His dancing in the rain was entertainment for the whole family. After a while he walked both kids out into the rain. They quickly became accustomed to the cold drops and began to enjoy themselves as they mimicked their father, both when they were dressed and when they were naked.

Mary was next to join in the fun. Josh noticed black water dripping from her skirt as the soot was rinsed away. Eventually she took off her clothes and hung them on branches of a dead tree out in the rain alongside of Josh's and the kid's clothes. Her cavorting was more than entertaining for Josh. His need for her was apparent.

Back under the rock, they dried the kids and put dry clothes on them. They tucked them into bed for a nap and then began drying each other. Josh kissed and licked away most of the moisture off Mary, as she did the same for him. They used the same old shirt they had used on the kids to dry them and finished drying themselves before they had wild, urgent sex over and over again. They never noticed when it stopped raining.

The kids needed new clothes, as what they wore was very tight and uncomfortable. There were holes in the knees. Their camp was a good spot. The rocks would absorb heat from the sun and from their fire. They would aid in keeping them warm at night. He could block the back to make the area more of a cave. He decided to set up a more permanent camp.

He went hunting and brought home two deer. He built a drying rack to dry and smoke the meat as Mary scraped the hide clean of hair. They used gall and brain matter rubbed into the hide to tenderize and tan it. They pounded the hides for hours with rocks.

Josh teased Mary that if she were a true Indian woman, she would chew the hide with her teeth to make it very soft. Mary did not like that idea at all. Eventually after a time, they started making clothes. Once they were outfitted with the new clothes, the children were much more comfortable. With a new supply of jerky and new clothes for the kids they relaxed for another day before proceeding.

CHAPTER 18

All rested up and relaxed, they continued on their way. The family enjoyed trooping through the woods to new adventures. The traveling grew less difficult, and they entered a very wide valley. Josh was sure there must be a town of some kind within a few miles.

They were watching for smoke or any sign of habitation but found none. They camped once more in a small glen in the forest. It had been a long day, and the children were tired. Josh and Mary stayed up for a while looking at the stars. A full moon lighted the night enough for them to see animals as they walked past the camp. Some stopped to sniff around, but none bothered them or seemed frightened by their presence.

The next morning they ate a leisurely breakfast and dawdled around for a while. The sun was shining brightly when they went on down the valley.

When they sighted a building, they were very excited and quickened their pace. They came into a short overgrown street with buildings on both sides. They could see houses scattered about, but most were in an advanced state of decay, as were the buildings on the street. They had found a ghost town. The business section consisted of four buildings, two on each side of the street that was less than a block long. It must have been a small settlement.

Josh cautiously entered one building that must have been a grocery or general merchandise establishment. Another across the street proved to be an old saloon. They never figured out what could have been in the other buildings. The kids had never seen a building to recognize one and were full of curiosity and wonder. They bounced up and down on the board sidewalk, enjoying the sound. A board broke under Little Josh, and his leg was scraped as his foot went through to the ground below. Mary jumped to his rescue and placed her foot on the boards. As she lifted Little Josh, her foot went through and landed more or less on its edge because of a rock under the walkway. She had twisted her ankle.

She removed her boot to massage her ankle. Immediately the ankle began to swell up. The pain almost made her cry. Josh had just exited the saloon with a small bottle in his hand. He was about to joke that the people of the old town had left them a bottle when he saw his wife sit down and remove her boot. The bottle in his hand was actually a bottle of liniment. He poured some of the foul smelling liquid on her ankle and rubbed it in. It helped the pain a little but actually did nothing for the injury.

While inspecting her ankle, he noticed twin little sets of holes that could only mean one thing. Some kind of snake had bitten her. Josh tore away the boardwalk and discovered a rattlesnake. His Bowie was suddenly in his hand and then flying through the air. It severed the snake's head. He cut Mary's ankle to make it bleed. Then he put a tourniquet on her leg, picked her up and carried her to where they had dropped their packs. He explained to Mary what had happened. He warned her to remain calm but told her she would be very sick for a time. At first she was frightened, but he assured her that very seldom did anyone die from a rattlesnake bite. Those who did usually had a bad heart to begin with so the poison was too much for them.

They knew there would be no traveling for a while so Josh quickly inspected the nearest buildings and chose the sturdiest of the bunch. The floor seemed solid, and it did not look as though the roof leaked much. There were only holes where windows once were, but there may never have been actual windows in the holes in the first place. Most pioneers used thin cloth, soaked in wax as windows. The room had a divider that consisted of a stove in one room and a fireplace in the other, right behind the stove. A work counter and cupboards were beside the stove. On the fireplace side there were bookshelves from floor to ceiling, and there were a number of books. The stovepipe and the stone chimney were intact. The room was about fifteen feet square on one side and twelve or so on the other side. The opening between the rooms was wide enough to consider it all one room. So the family had plenty of space.

After spreading out their bed on the floor, he carried Mary in his arms over the threshold and placed her on their bed. He commented, "Carrying you over thresholds is getting to be a habit I like."

It would be a while before Mary would get over the snakebite. She was feverish, and her ankle was doubly swelled from the sprain and the poison. Josh first soaked dried potatoes and then mashed them. He put a thick layer of the potatoes over her wound and ankle. He held it in place with buckskin. As the potatoes dried, they pulled poison out of her system and aided in helping the swelling go down.

He knew Mary would suffer for several days before she would begin to recover. By the time she would be strong enough to walk, the sprain would be healed. The main concern was the snakebite.

Josh was in a quandary. He knew the herbs to gather for an old Indian remedy to take down her fever and to counteract the poison. The problem was that in order to get them, he would have to leave the babies alone to do it quickly. If he took them with him, it would take longer, and Mary would suffer.

The dog was guarding the children while playing with them. If they approached the boardwalk or building, he would get between their destination and them. He would gently guide them away from the danger he perceived. Josh could see that they were getting tired, so he laid them beside their mother and told her he was going to get medicine. The dog got comfortable beside the kids. She was awake and coherent, but the fever was just starting to tire her.

Josh went hunting while the twins took their nap. He was back in less than an hour with a deer over his shoulder and herbs stuffed into his shirt. He got a fire going, fetched water from the river and washed the leaves and roots he had collected. He crushed them and put them in water to boil. After a time, he could smell the concoction and did not like the smell. He threw in some mint leaves and let it boil some more. It smelled minty when he took it off the fire. He added cold water to cool it down.

By this time Mary was burning with fever and was off in the

world of fever-induced dreams. When the medicine was cool enough, he lifted her up and poured some of the tea in her mouth. Some of it dribbled out, but she automatically swallowed a lot. Shortly afterward she seemed to sleep a little better.

The one application of mashed potatoes did all the good such a remedy could do. It drew out all the venom that had not washed away from the cuts Josh had made or had entered her blood stream.

The old story of sucking out the poison being a good thing to do is not true, and Josh knew it. Mostly all it does is make the person who tried it sick from a small amount of venom that his system absorbed in his mouth. There is no need for a direct entrance through an infected tooth or sore. The inside of the mouth really absorbs it without any help.

All Josh could do was to give her some of the medicinal tea about every hour and about three times a day give her broth from the stew he had cooking constantly on the stove. His main chore of course was the twins. They understood that mommy was sick. Although the term was new to them, they did not try to play with her or wake her. Their dog Candy took over babysitting.

Josh knew it would be a long time before Mary would regain her strength so he began to prepare for winter. He could not leave the house except for short periods because she might need him. From books and experience he knew she would probably be in a coma for at least three days and would be in bed or barely able to move about for at least a month. She would tire very quickly and would sleep a lot. By spring she would be back to her old self.

As Josh remembered reading about what Indians did for snakebite, he gave Mary her tea every day for a week. It took her out of the fever and induced a comatose state where she slept comfortably.

There was no need to construct an outhouse since there was one already there. Josh installed the airplane toilet seat mostly because he had it and a little bit out of habit.

He lucked out as far as meat for the table was concerned. The livestock in the area was not used to people inhabiting the old town. Deer and elk wandered into town frequently. Rabbits lived under the houses, and there were plenty of them about. Josh actually never had to go hunting. He shot much of their winter supply off the porch of their new home. He dressed his kills and left the entrails out for the wolves and coyotes. They never failed to clean up after him.

He did have a little time while the kids slept in the afternoon, and his wife started sleeping normally. He wandered about until he found various vegetables now growing wild. He harvested most of them and dried them. He built an elaborate drying rack and had meat almost constantly drying into jerky. He dried the vegetables in the heat of the sun on a large flat rock.

Eventually Mary was able to hobble around a little with Josh's help. This helped a lot. She was able, with help, to make it out to the outhouse and back. She could take care of herself and feed herself. Josh built her a crutch to help her. As expected, she could only be up for a few minutes before she went back to bed and slept for hours.

Josh jerked meat and used buckskin to make a new shirt. Carrying a big load all that time and living the way they did had buffed him up to where his shoulders and chest were much bigger. The buckskin shirt he made while his leg was broken would not fit any more. He felt he would need to be wearing a shirt when they reached civilization. He had not worn a shirt since the last of the snow left in the spring. He was so brown with suntan from the waist up that he looked like a red-headed Indian.

When Josh made Mary's skirt, she had just delivered the twins and still had somewhat of a stomach. She was now the slim and trim girl she was before the pregnancy. Her skirt was too big around. He took four inches off the waist of both of her skirts. She was saving one that was very clean for their arrival. She also had a pair of her panties secreted away. She had "gone commando" for two years for the most part except during "that time."

In investigating around the old buildings for things they might use, Josh came across a suitcase hidden behind and under an old counter. It looked fairly new. Josh set it on top of the counter and opened it. It was full of Canadian money.

Josh took the suitcase back to their quarters and set it down. He told Mary to be careful because someone might come back for that money. The dust on the floor of the building showed no footprints so he knew the money had been there for quite some time. He determined that he would not leave his family alone for any length of time even after Mary got to feeling better. He determined to be vigilant.

CHAPTER 19

Winter came early or so it seemed. It snowed about the first of September and stayed. There was no Indian summer. Josh had everything prepared and was ready. He covered the windows against the cold and let the light from the fireplace illuminate the room. He explored until he found some old curtains that would hold together. He found wax in an old gallon can. He found a big iron kettle that could hang on a hook in their fireplace. The hook was on a swivel and the kettle could be swung in and out either over the fire or out, so it could be accessed. He cleaned the kettle and had a stew going at all times. He waxed the sheer curtains and made "window glass." He found an old bedstead and an old table and chairs. He used layers of hides for a mattress on the bed. He furnished the house with things he brought from other houses in the town. He found several of the old two-gallon cans with kerosene in them and several old kerosene lamps. He ended up with five full cans and one partial.

He placed a chair beside Mary at her side of the bed. Josh read to Mary and the children from the old books off the bookcase. Josh would hold her hand and read. The twins thought they should do the same and held each other's hand. Sometimes Mary slept while he read. From the beginning, he would test her temperature by kissing her forehead. He showed her all the tenderness and love he could to encourage her and let her know she was needed. The twins frequently kissed her, generally on the forehead or cheek. When Mary was out of bed, she spent hours in an old rocking chair and read aloud to Josh and the children. The twins would sit at her feet, and Josh would lean back on the bed.

There was a McGuffey reader that the kids loved. At less than three, they began to learn to read. Mary's illness began to leave, and she gained strength on a daily basis. By the time Josh thought it was Christmas again, she cooked a big roast for Christmas dinner. She was nearly back to her old self. For a

Christmas present she told Josh she was ready to be intimate again.

Josh's wandering around in the old buildings had netted him some toys. He had dolls for Little Mary with changes of clothes, a toy rifle and toy pistol for Little Josh and for the two of them, a wagon. He cleaned their presents carefully and the night before Christmas set them under a tree he brought in and decorated with ribbons he made from old cloth scraps he had found.

Of course the children were delighted, and the Christmas story was told. Other stories were read from one of the books that included other Christmas stories.

Spring came at its usual time after a month-long fight with Old Man Winter to determine dominance. Spring, of course, won as winter retreated to come again in about five months.

They began to plan their interrupted journey to seek civilization. They were sure it would be only a few days' journey at most, so they did not hurry.

It was over a week later, and Mary was outside getting some sun while the twins took their nap. Josh had gone hunting for their evening meal.

A jeep came into town with two men in it. They spotted Mary right away and stopped near her. Instead of being glad to see people, she was frightened. Something about the men made her very uneasy.

There was no greeting of any kind. One of the men said, "Woman, get your clothes off and lay down; me and my friend Verge here are going to fuck you hard. I get you first, and when I am through, Verge will fuck you. When he is through, I will do you again, and we will keep doing you as long as we want. When we get through, we may keep you around as a toy for a few days."

Verge looked into the house and saw the twins sleeping. He told her, "Do as Roy says or I'll bash your brats' heads in and then rape your ass."

Mary knew they meant every word, but she could not speak,

she was so scared. Roy pulled out an Arkansas Toothpick, a dagger-shaped knife, and split her blouse open right up the front. He was not too careful and nicked her a little. He then cut away at her skirt until it dropped to the ground. She was completely naked once Verge came up from behind her and pulled her top back and off.

Josh witnessed the cutting away of her clothes as he approached. He put his hand down in a gesture to tell Candy to sit. Back in his college days, he had won the world archery championship by shooting two arrows so rapidly at two different targets that it seemed he shot both at the same time. In fact, some who saw it swore he did. He hit the bull's eye on both targets. He notched one arrow and held the second in his teeth. Mary was backing away, and the men were laughing at her as they stood near each other and started stripping. It was a perfect shot for Josh. He pulled back the bowstring as far as he could stretch it and released and then released again.

One arrow entered Roy's chest, went through his heart and was sticking out the back. Verge never realized what happened because the second arrow went all the way through his neck severing both jugulars. Both men dropped to the ground. Verge was bleeding to death, and Roy was dead.

Josh ignored the two bodies and went straight to his wife. He held her as she trembled and took some time to calm herself down. She said, "They were going to kill my babies, and they were going to rape me and use me. Who are those horrible men?"

Josh told her, "I suspect they are the ones who hid that suitcase full of money." It took time and patience to further calm Mary. He guided her into the house and put her on the bed, holding her. By the time she calmed down, she fell asleep in Josh's arms. She slept for two hours.

Josh loaded the bodies over the hood of the jeep and was going to take them out and dump them when he thought better of it. He decided to leave them hung over the hood.

He was considering what had happened. The best thing was that jeep. They had transportation; there must be a road of some kind that led to somewhere, and somewhere probably meant a settlement of some kind. He hoped everyone in the town was not like the two representatives he had over the hood.

CHAPTER 20

The next morning they loaded the jeep with their belongings. The twins rode on their mother's lap. The family started on their way.

Josh told Mary, "If I did not know that we will be going to a safe and quiet haven, I would be tempted to go back to the Ritz Cave and live there. We found a town, granted it is a ghost town, but it is civilization in a way. The first thing Little Josh scrapes his leg, and then you twist an ankle and are bitten by a snake. Then two fine examples of manhood try to rape you and murder our children. That is some introduction to civilization!"

Josh drove easily and cautiously over very rough roads and many times was happy that the jeep was a four-wheel drive. Candy ran along beside the vehicle. At one point they saw a sloppy campsite and knew the two had camped there. They drove all day until dusk and still did not reach a town. They camped, ate dinner, and slept.

The jeep's trail led through the forest where there was no discernible road at times and a narrow rutted trail at others. He could see where Verge and Roy had driven around fallen trees and rocks in the old road. Josh stayed in the tracks made when the two came into the old town. At one point he noticed that the jeep was almost out of gas. He found that one of the two jeep cans, one on either side of the jeep, was full. Verge and Roy had prepared for their return journey. He emptied it into the gas tank and continued. He knew he was about five gallons away from a town or less.

Late in the afternoon they finally came to where the old wagon trail met another road. This road was one that looked traveled. It was gravel and it was maintained. They camped in the woods for the night. Josh went down the road a ways and saw nothing. Reversing, he went about a mile past their camp. He saw a sign that said something about a restaurant five kilometers ahead. He hurried back to his family to report. She had dinner ready, and so he told them while they ate that they would be in civilization in the morning.

They had to explain what civilization was to the twins. Mary told them, "There will be people and houses, stores where we can buy clothes instead of making our own, different kinds of food and kids your own age to play with. Do you think you would like that? The two heard the enthusiasm in their mother's voice and quickly agreed.

Mary could hardly sleep, and for the very first time she was up earlier than Josh. She shook him and told him, "Wake up, you big lummox, we have to get ready. This is an important day in our lives."

Josh kissed her good morning and said, "What is so special about today? Is it because I plan to take you out for breakfast?"

She hit his shoulder and told him, "Enough of your malarkey; get up and heat some water. I am going to take a bath, and so is everyone else." It took two hours to get the water heated and everyone spruced up. She combed and brushed her hair and his. She spent a half hour fussing over the twins. She cut some of the over two years' growth from Josh's hair and tied it in a ponytail. She did the same with Little Josh's hair.

At last she was ready. "Ok, now you can take us out to breakfast." They loaded the jeep and started up. Just as they were about to pull onto the road, a pick-up truck drove by. The couple in the truck stared at them and then speeded up.

Once on the road Josh told Mary, "I think it would be a good idea to visit a police station first, don't you?"

With a twinkle in her eye, she told him, "Well, it could relieve the jeep of some of its load and might attract less attention that way. So I suppose we can make that one stop if you insist. Just remember the twins are hungry, and so am I, so no lollygagging."

They were met at the edge of town by a boy of about twelve. He yelled something at them and started running down the road in front of them. Candy took a place beside the boy and ran with him. The boy would wave his arm as a signal to follow him. Josh slowed down and followed the kid. People stared and began to follow the jeep. Other boys joined the first. It was a virtual parade. When they got to the police station, the only policeman in town was standing in front of the building. The boy stopped, turned, and took a bow while swinging his arms as though to present the officer and saying, "Here we are."

Josh slammed on the brakes to keep from hitting the boy. Both bodies went off the front of the jeep and landed face up side by side. The officer came over and looked at their faces. He nodded his head and gestured for Josh to come in to the station. When Josh was seated, he said, "Tell me about it."

Before Josh could speak, Mary and the children entered. She said, "So many people, and the twins are frightened. Why do they keep staring at us? They just keep staring and talking among themselves."

The officer told her, "It is probably because it is not every day that a family brings in two bodies draped like deer over the hood of their jeep, especially two of the most wanted fugitives in the whole province. Now I need to know all the details for my report, if you please."

Josh gave him the details about the killing and capture of the two. The officer thanked him and asked, "Where do you want the reward sent, or do you want to accompany me to the bank and collect it?"

Josh told him, "What I want is to take my family out to breakfast and a hotel room. I need to call the FAA, or whatever you call the aeronautics people here, and report an airplane crash. Officer, if you would like, we will come back and tell you the rest of our story."

The policeman said, "I am sorry; my name is Bradbury Singleton. I forgot to introduce myself in all the excitement. If you do not mind, call me Brad. I will go over to the bank while you go across the street and eat. I will meet you there with the reward money. Tell Louise to give you the special table. It is private, and you will be able to eat in peace."

When they stepped outside, the crowd was still there. The two bodies had not been moved, and people were taking pictures of them. One young man asked if they minded his

103

taking their picture. Josh said they did not mind at all and let the picture be taken. The man handed Josh a card. He was a reporter. Josh looked at the card and said, "Mister Young, you were polite enough to ask, so I will ask you. Would you like a shot at the Pulitzer?"

He replied, "Call me Larry, and of course I would. Every reporter would like one."

Josh told him, "Have I got a story for you! Come with us and keep your mouth shut until I invite you to speak. You can make notes or you can record, but do not ask any questions until you hear the whole story. Agreed?"

Upon entering the restaurant, they were greeted by an older, buxom woman who introduced herself as Louise. She took them to the private table and wrote down their order. Both Josh and Mary ordered ham and eggs with coffee. Larry also ordered breakfast. For the children it was pancakes and eggs. Louise brought the coffee shortly with glasses of milk for the twins.

Everything the twins ate was new to them, but instead of rejecting things, they ate and drank until their little tummies were bulging. Mary spent some time making sure they ate properly.

They tried to act as though dining out was an everyday occurrence, but their excitement was apparent. Larry sat nearby and listened intently. Constable Brad came in and noticed that Josh had a suitcase on the floor beside him.

He said, "You would not have recovered their loot, too, did you?" Josh told him it so happened that he did find a suitcase full of money. He did not know if it were the "loot" or not since the men never said.

Brad told him, "There is a sizeable reward for the recovery of that money. The bank has offered one hundred thousand for its return and the capture of the men who shot and killed three of their employees and four customers."

Josh asked if there were any wrappers on the bundles and what bank. He was told the correct information. He opened the suitcase and took out one hundred thousand dollars in cash. He wrote a receipt on a piece of paper Larry handed him and put it in the suitcase. He told Brad, "I do not trust bankers I do not know, so I have taken my reward and given them a receipt."

Brad said, "Thank you, Josh; you are a smart man. I will take this to the bank and just let them try to delay paying the reward the province offered for Roy and Verge. I was about to tell you it would be an hour or so before they will have your money ready. Did I mention it is the same bank that those two robbed?

"There is a thriving lumber industry here, and they hit the bank on payday so there was a lot of cash on hand to use in cashing the payroll checks."

After they finished breakfast, Josh told the story from beginning to end. He left out the intimate details that were no one's business. He did not mention that they were anything other than a man and wife when the airplane crashed.

He started with flight 6969 and ended with their entrance into town. It took two hours for the story to unfold. Constable Brad went to report the plane crash and the finding of two survivors. Larry, the reporter, sat there thinking. Suddenly he stood up and stared at Josh. He almost shouted, "Josh McDougal? You are Josh McDougal? Oh My God! Oh my God!" He ran from the restaurant.

Josh told his family, "I guess he is going to report. He is a reporter after all."

Mary was looking at Josh strangely, "The way he said your name. It sounded as though he knew something about you that is important."

He just said, "Yes, it did. I wonder why."

They asked Louise where the hotel was located in the town. She told them, "We don't have a hotel, but you are welcome to come to my house. I have plenty of room and have not had little ones around the place for nearly ten years. I would like that. Besides, I owe you; my husband was killed in that robbery."

Josh would not hear her when she told him the meal was on the house. He did not argue; he thanked her and left a hundred-dollar "tip" on the table. Brad came back as they were leaving and handed Josh an envelope full of money. He said, "I counted it twice; all twenty-five thousand is there. They wanted to charge you a transaction fee until I told them you were smarter than that."

CHAPTER 21

They were taken to Louise's house by the young guide who turned out to be Louise's grandson, Tom. Candy was still with Tom and seemed to have adopted him. Josh told Tom, "Would you like that dog? His name is Candy because he is a lifesaver." Tom caught on to the inference immediately and laughed. He was more than happy to give Candy a home.

Louise had told them they were to take the first bedroom on the left and put the twins in the next one because there was a connecting door. Louise said her bedroom was across the hall from theirs. They drove the jeep over and unloaded what they needed. Mary and the twins stayed there while Josh went to try to make some arrangements to get back home and to report to Brad.

The Constable was on the phone when Josh walked in. He heard Brad make a remark, "Here, let him tell you himself." He handed the phone to Josh. Josh spent nearly an hour on the telephone with the various officials of the airline and the government. He agreed to meet with them and hung up.

Josh inquired about the jeep. He was told it belonged to Verge, and as far as the Constable was concerned, it now belonged to Josh. He wrote out a title transfer and told Josh to stop into the province office and have it transferred. Josh did as asked since the province office was next door. While there, he took care of another transaction. He obtained a marriage license that was backdated to the day of the crash. It was stamped, registered, and made legal. He was such a hero to the whole area that they would do almost anything for him.

He obtained birth certificates for the twins with everything filled in. The doctor helped count the days on the tally stick and backdated the calendar to the correct date. Josh gave him the time of births. He brought in his "hidden treasure" and set it out. They measured the length of the twins on the sticks he produced. They weighed the rocks Josh had marked and carried so far. Little Josh weighed 6 pounds and 8 ounces. Little Mary weighed just 4 ounces less. Little Josh was officially named Josh McDougal Jr. and Little Mary was given the name of Mary Ann McDougal. They would forever be Little Josh and Little Mary in their parents' eyes.

He met Larry on the street and filled him in. Larry handed him a newspaper. He said, "This story is in every newspaper in the world with my byline. I can smell that Pulitzer right now, and I want to thank you, sir."

Josh told him, "You wrote the story and did not try to sensationalize it and lie. You did it right, and you deserve that prize if anyone ever did. Don't thank me; thank your parents for raising you to be polite." He left Larry deep in thought.

Josh purchased new store-bought clothes for the whole family at the mercantile, got a haircut and headed home. He showed Mary their marriage certificate and the two birth certificates. She was thrilled. The clothes he bought fit well, and they changed out of their buckskins. The twins were dressed as any other children. Mary would not let Josh change until he bathed thoroughly and washed his hair. It felt good to soap down and let the shower rinse the lather away.

Mary noticed the folded newspaper Josh had casually tossed on a table and opened it. The headline was large and covered the upper half of the paper.

"WORLD FAMOUS MOUNTAINEER RESCUES FAIR LADY." She went on to read that Josh McDougal was actually a world famous mountain man and had published several books dealing with survival skills in the wilderness, as well as "what to do" books about survival. He was the ultimate authority on the subject. He was also a professor of mathematics at the University of Montana. She was speechless.

Mary stormed into the bathroom waving the newspaper and told him he was full of Blarney and was nothing but a spreader of malarkey. That was the essence of what she said, but it took her several minutes to say it.

When she started to wind down, Josh just looked at her and told her, "Mary, You didn't tell me everything either. You never mentioned that you are the daughter of one of the richest men in

Ireland and that you have your doctorate in economics. I only told you part of my story, and you only told me part of yours. We are even."

She began to laugh. "I always knew there was more to you than you let on. I just did not know it was this much.

What else did you neglect to tell me?"

He told her, "Wait until you see the house" and let the subject drop.

Mary's parents flew in by helicopter the next morning. Brad dropped by and told them the time to expect their arrival. There were two vacant lots next to the province offices that made a good place to land. One of the things Josh did at the Constable's office was to ask the airline to let Mary's parents know their daughter was alive and well. Josh and Mary met them with the twins hiding behind their mother. They didn't know what to think of that flying machine.

After a warm greeting, Mary introduced Josh by saying, "This handsome Irishman is an American and is my husband Josh McDougal. Here behind me is Little Josh and Little Mary, our twins."

As the two men shook hands, Josh looked up and said, "I think we had better move if we expect to talk. It is going to be noisy here very shortly. There must have been a dozen helicopters above them waiting to land. There were more in the distance, and all were expecting to land. They moved down the street to the restaurant. Louise seated them at the special table so they could talk.

Brad put two men to work directing air traffic and helping the helicopters unload and take off quickly. They worked a system of bringing them in from one side and taking off in the opposite direction. It worked efficiently.

They watched as helicopter after helicopter landed and deposited news crews from every major network, and a few not major. Larry was right there greeting each of them as news cameras ground away. His face would be on every newscast because he was the one with the story, and he saw to it that he got plenty of footage. News cameras filmed every square inch of the town, and eventually the news people started to enter the restaurant. They were told to order food or get out. Louise was not about to let them take up room if they were not paying for the space. Most of them were hungry anyway and ordered a meal.

Mary's parents were expecting to greet a starved and emancipated daughter who would need care and time to recuperate. The healthy, vibrant daughter they found was a pleasant surprise. They expected that the man with her had used her and were fully ready to prosecute him.

They saw immediately from the pride and tone in her voice that their daughter loved Josh and was proud to be his wife. Josh told how he had arranged for their marriage to be the day of the crash. The marriage certificate even stated that the pilot as captain of the craft had performed the ceremony. The two of them told Mr. and Mrs. McIntosh the true story. It was a story that would only be repeated once, when they told their children on their eighteenth birthday.

They fell in love with the twins. Josh told them they should say hello to their grandmother and grandfather. Almost in one voice they asked, "What is a grandmother? What is a grandfather?" The relationship was explained to them.

Mary was asked, "You have a mommy and a daddy just like us?"

She assured them that she did, and they were right there. She pointed and said, "This lady is my mommy, and this man is my daddy."

Larry arranged with Josh to have a meeting with the press using the front porch of the restaurant as a stage since it was about two feet off the ground. Josh and Mary stood before the crowd with her mother and father behind, holding the twins up so they could see.

Josh told the crowd, "I gave the complete story to Larry. Anything you wish to know he can tell you. If you need further information, wait until I publish the book." Someone asked if it had been difficult with a rank novice along and his having to lead her out of the mountains. Josh told the reporter that if he did some homework, he would know that he had taken hundreds out into the wilds and taught them survival. "Actually she was about the best pupil I have ever had."

A question was asked as to when the couple had married and how they met. Josh told them, "That is an interesting story. I was on the airplane and in my seat when the flight attendant escorted this young, beautiful woman to the seat beside me. I was in love at first sight. I told her I would only let her sit there if she were my wife. I do not know why, but she agreed, so the Captain of the airship performed the ceremony then and there."

A reporter from a major scandal sheet called out, "Did you consummate the union then and there with everyone watching?"

To that very rude question, Josh answered, "None of your business."

The reporter shouted out, "I was not asking you; I was asking her. Can't she speak for herself?"

Josh stepped aside and Mary stepped forward, "I am Mrs. Josh McDougal. What was your question, sir?" He called it out again and Mary answered, "None of your business." She stepped back. The crowd cheered and clapped.

Josh noticed two men who did not fit in with the crowd of reporters and townspeople. One wore a suit and the other a uniform. Josh nodded to them from the front before starting to speak. After Mary put the rude person in his place, they went back into the café as reporters and camera crews inundated Larry with questions.

The two men Josh had noticed followed them into the restaurant. They were the officials from the airline and the government.

A large topographical map was spread out on the table. Josh traced their route back through the ghost town, the disappearing river, and on up into the wilderness. At last he tapped a spot on the map. "You will find what is left of the airplane right here. You can land a chopper about a hundred yards to the south of the wreckage. If you do a fly-over, you should see the reflection of a piece of wing I set up for that purpose before we left. I set it to reflect the sun and act as a marker." They wrote down both Mary's and Josh's statements and both signed the papers. Josh told them where and how to contact them if there were further questions.

Josh and the others were told that the section of the aircraft that fell and ultimately caused the crash was found and analyzed. They could find no reason for the crash except that the wing section near one of the engines had hit something very hard. They asked about the elevation, and Josh told them that the pilot had announced earlier that they would be flying at thirty thousand feet. After the accident or whatever it was happened, they were forced to go down to ten thousand feet, according to the information Josh had heard over the airplane's intercom. It was a complete mystery what could have hit the airplane thirty thousand feet in the air. There were no reports of other aircraft down at the time.

The rude reporter came into the restaurant as the officials were leaving. Louise met him just inside the door and told him to leave. He started giving her trouble, but Brad stepped in. Brad was well over six feet tall and had shoulders that would make a bulldogger jealous. He looked down at the man and told him to get out and also get out of town. He said, "We don't need your kind here so get out of town before I throw you in jail."

The reporter began to argue and said he had a right to ask questions and a right to be there because he was a certified reporter. Brad said, "I am the law here. It happens that I am a little more certified than you are. I saw you out in the middle of the street. I have you for impeding traffic in a public street, loitering, verbal assault, riotous behavior, and I will be able to think of some more if you give me time. You leave within ten minutes, or I will take you in and lock you up. I sincerely hope you resist arrest." The man was gone in half the time.

In order to avoid the reporters, Louise showed the four

adults and two children out the back. They went to Louise's house and talked for hours. Of course, they had to go over every detail of their meeting and courtship again. When Mary was through with her side of the story, both of her parents accepted Josh and were proud of having him in their family. They accepted Josh's invitation to come and spend a few days at the McDougal ranch, as he called it.

During the night Josh, Mary, the twins and both of her parents boarded her father's leased helicopter and left. Just before they left, Josh signed the title to the jeep over to Louise. They knew Candy was safe with Tom as his new friend.

They packed and took with them the airplane toilet seat, the old miner's gold, and the Bowie knife. Josh still had his "hidden treasure." Of course, they took their buckskin clothes. Louise promised to ship some of the bear rugs and the one cougar pelt. Everything else was given to Louise to do with as she pleased.

They landed at an airport and finished the journey in a private luxury jet leased to Mary's father through his company. Josh exchanged his Canadian currency for American and deposited it in a trust for his children's education. He sold the gold through a broker friend and persuaded a friend to drive them all out to the ranch.

The sign over the gate read, "McDougal's Blarney Ranch." When Mary saw the house, her only comment was, "It figures."